PRAISE FOR BARSK

"A work of singular imaginative power. It's a delight from beginning to end."

—**Walter Jon Williams**, Nebula Award-winning author of *The Green Leopard Plague*

"Powerful. Grand in scope, yet deeply intimate."

—**Howard Tayler**, Hugo Award-winning creator of *Schlock Mercenary*

"A heartfelt and wonderfully weird book: a space opera about kindness and memory."

—**Max Gladstone**, author of *Craft Sequence*

<u>Also by Lawrence M. Schoen:</u>

The Universe of Barsk

Barsk: The Elephants' Graveyard
Moons of Barsk
Excerpts of Jorl ben Tral

The Amazing Conroy

Buffalito Bundle
Barry's Tale
Calendrical Regression
Barry's Deal
Buffalito Destiny
Trial of the Century
Buffalito Contingency

Freelance Courier

Ace of Corpses
Ace of Saints
Ace of Thralls

Pizza in Space

Slice of Entropy
Slice of Chaos

Pirates of Sol

Pirates of Marz
Pirates of Earth

SOUP OF THE MOMENT

A Tale of BARSK

Lawrence M. Schoen

GUARDBRIDGE BOOKS
ST ANDREWS, SCOTLAND

Published by Guardbridge Books,
St Andrews, Fife, United Kingdom.
http://guardbridgebooks.co.uk

Soup Of The Moment.
(Revised Edition)

This is a work of fiction. All characters and events portrayed in
this book are fictitious, and any resemblance to real people or
events is purely coincidental.

ISBN: 978-1-911486-79-4

This one is for Sydney,
because creatives,
regardless of their medium,
need others to chat with.

The Lovers

"PEOPLE CAN'T FLY. And if you think they can, you're either crazy or practicing a bedtime story for your nieces and nephews." Gavi stomped his foot and trumpeted less than an ear's breadth from Pholo's face.

She turned from him, casting her gaze across the tiny table that served as center space of the courtyard before the entrance to Gavi's bachelor apartment. Bindle, seated opposite, refused to meet Pholo's eyes, choosing instead to shake her head in disapproval. Great. Both of her lovers were against her.

And both were wrong.

"People fly all the time," said Pholo, her voice not so much calm as devoid of emotion. At times like this, though she wanted to grow old with him, she didn't much like Gavi. He could be so rigid, so conventional. He was going to grow into a great physician, at least for those patients whose ailments and maladies fell within the established parameters of medical science. And Bindle, normally brilliant and bright as a flutterby, Bindle whose words could make audiences weep or cheer or cry out in the grip of unknown emotion, her utter silence hit Pholo harder than any blow. How could she argue with Bindle when the woman chose not to speak?

And yet, she loved them both. Maybe not as deeply as Gavi adored her, or as passionately as Bindle burned for her, but that was just who she was. Curiously, one of the few things her lovers had in common was the intensity of their feelings for her. Both always gave of themselves fully. Pholo couldn't do that, she always had to hold something back with people. Not so with her research. Science had always come first and she poured everything into the work. Why couldn't she treat the people most important to her without reservation? Huh. Maybe for the same reason they couldn't see why this project was so important. If she could only make them understand, it would somehow grant her permission to give them more of herself in turn. With that reasoning in the back of her mind, she imagined her lovers were just confused seminar students and she tried a new approach.

"The rest of the Alliance flies every day, between islands and continents, in machines designed for that express purpose. And before they relocated every Lox and Eleph to this planet, our Fant ancestors flew right alongside them."

"But—"

Gavi tried to interrupt but she wasn't done and cut him off. "And what about the Patrol? The Patrol flies between worlds, in vessels that can withstand cold vacuum and blistering re-entry, and they've done so for millennia. Millennia! So don't you tell me people can't fly, Gavi. Maybe no one on Barsk does so, but we've been on this planet for only a few centuries. Before coming here, we didn't build our cities in island rainforests or live our entire lives never seeing anyone who wasn't a Fant."

"What's your point?"

"Our people were just like everyone else. We flew."

"Yes, with machines and ships."

With one heavily gloved hand she lifted what looked

like a trio of interconnected dinner plates from the satchel she'd placed on the table. She set them aside, reached in again and laid her flight goggles alongside the plates. The third time she took a small case from the satchel, and opened it to reveal the heart of her creation, the first working battery that would power her flight harness.

"*This* is a machine," she said even as Gavi slashed his trunk once again in negation. She wasn't going to shout, wasn't going to let her emotions carry her argument. But she wasn't going to stay silent. Bad enough he kept increasing his volume, almost in contrast to Bindle's continued quiet.

Gavi stomped again. "People fly *inside* machines, big ones. I've sailed from here to Belp, I know how big vessels can be, and the touring agent made each of us take a practice turn in a one-man emergency raft, so I know how small too. You're not talking about any kind of craft that you climb into, any kind of vessel that might keep you safe. Your machine is a device small enough to wear on a belt."

"Oh, you'd have more faith if I made it bigger and bulkier?"

"That's not what he's saying." Bindle broke her silence.

"No? Cuz that's what I'm hearing." The chill of Pholo's voice cut through their protests. Gavi's trunk fell flat against his chest as he dropped like a sack of wet laundry onto the bench. As if only one of the pair could be animated at a time, Bindle stirred and took Pholo's ungloved hand in both of hers.

"We're just... I'm scared for you, 'lo. Have you

discussed this with Maefis, your therapist? Gotten her opinion?"

That almost stopped her, where none of their own arguments had. But Bindle, usually so fierce, so indomitable, gazed up at her like a frightened child and in effect questioned her sanity. Damn.

"There's nothing to be scared of." She swiveled back and forth, looking for answers in their faces. "I showed both of you the math several tendays ago. Why are you freaking out now?"

"Because I'm a doctor, not an engineer," said Gavi. "I don't do much math, and what little I need is simple and applied, not the abstract work that drives your machine. And no, Pholo, don't try to walk me through it again. I couldn't follow half of it the last time, and now..." He paused and lifted the portable scanner he'd *borrowed* from the island's main clinic during his last shift, for no other reason than because she'd asked him. He stood, scanned the object in her gloved hand, and offered her the device, showing her the display. "Do you see? This tells us that your prototype has been drenched in radiation. And all this from just a test run with a dummy wearing the gear. If that had been you, how do you expect you'd survive it?"

Pholo pulled her hand from Bindle and turned from Gavi. She let the battery slip from her gloved hand, back into its shielded case before she stepped away from the table, retreating to the far end of the little courtyard so she could regard both of them at once. "I won't need to. The radiation is a side effect of the transduction process. The longer it takes, the more radiation you get."

Bindle understood first, her poet's brain making

intuitive leaps far faster than Gavi's pragmatism. Relief colored her voice as she asked, "You're saying you can speed things up? Charge it faster?"

"Oh yeah, easily. This was just a proof of concept. I had it set up on a long pole on top of an observation platform in the canopy, it absorbed the wind for two full tendays."

Gavi trumpeted again. "If you knew taking so long would cause so much radiation what did you—"

She cut him off. "Because given that amount of ordinary weather, that's how long it took to charge."

Bindle nodded, her ears flapping with new hope. "So if you could charge faster—"

"—there'd be little radiation, maybe none at all. I just need better, more severe, weather."

Gavi scowled. "Oh right, because severe weather is safer than exposure to radiation?"

"Can be," she said. "I've been thinking it through, and I believe the trick is to not be around anything that the weather can use to hurt me."

It was Bindle's turn to stomp. Did they have rules to their turn taking? They knew about one another of course, her aunts had taught her that open and honest communication was critical to making any relationship work, let alone two. But she rarely spent time with both of them at once. She couldn't recall the last time they'd been together, all three of them.

"You've lost me," said Bindle. "What does that even mean?"

"Tell us both," said Gavi.

And just like that, having shown that she'd actually heard and addressed their repeated concerns, Pholo knew she'd won them over. They loved her, worried about her, but they also understood that her work defined her; they wanted to be convinced, for her sake as well as theirs. She drew close and took Bindle's hand back in hers. She twined her trunk with Gavi's. "It's simple. I plan to charge it away from this island. So no matter how fierce the winds, there'll be no soil or trees or anything else it might throw at me."

"What, you're planning on being out at sea on a boat? Where you can be hit with giant waves, or plunged beneath, or smashed by them until your boat splinters and each piece is a weapon to be used against you?" Gavi pulled his trunk free and even Bindle let go of her hand.

"Now who's telling bedtime stories?"

"Pholo, please, we're serious. Gavi and I want to help, we want you to succeed, but not at the cost of your health or life. Trying to charge your device on the open sea isn't safer than on our island."

"I know. I never said I was going out on a boat." Pholo snapped the nubs of her trunk at Gavi. "You said that."

"Then how?"

"I'm going to fly above it. I'll charge it in the open air."

Gavi looked like he wanted to tear off his own ears in frustration. "But you can't. Even if your machine worked, you couldn't use it to fly before you charge it, and you're saying you need to fly in order to charge it."

"To charge the finished version, not the prototype. Like I said, that was just a proof of concept. It works, it charged, but it has only a fraction of the power I'll need to really fly."

"But—"

"It has enough to get me up there, into the heart of some serious weather."

"Up where? And how serious?"

"Well… Maybe instead of 'heart' I should have said 'eye'."

Her lovers gasped in tandem. "No."

"Yes!"

"That's crazy!"

"As to that, I can't really say. But if I'm to properly charge my device, quickly enough to prevent the radiation backwash, — and yes, I acknowledge that is a real concern — then I need to do so in the eye of a hurricane."

Gavi sputtered, his mouth hanging open, like he'd lost the ability to speak. And Bindle, with a performer's timing and sense of the dramatic, fainted dead away.

The Grandmother

PHOLO SHARED her home with six generations. It was a sprawling household, one of the largest on the island of Kelprey with almost one hundred children from the youngest generation. Her generation had several dozen siblings and cousins of varying degrees. Her mother's included twenty-seven aunts, with thirteen grandmothers and great-aunts in the generation before that, who answered to eight great-grandmothers. Pholo's great-great-grandmother, an ancient woman — the oldest on the island — named Salaphora but whom everyone called Granny Rosie, still ran the house, as she had for more than twice as long as any of her predecessors.

In her youth Salaphora had been a chef. Her father had been a traveling salesman, his territory the entire Western Archipelago. Salaphora had adored the man. His infrequent visits home included tales of meals on far away islands, and the savory treats he'd brought back wrapped in aromatic leaves had shaped her career choice, despite the wishes of her mother and aunts.

Perhaps as a gesture of accountability, or maybe simply to waggle his trunk at her mother's household, Salaphora's father had paid her tuition to culinary school. She'd specialized in soups, developing recipes that no one within tendays of Kelprey had ever experienced, drawing heavily on the remembered flavors of her father's presents. The rose petal soup she devised, made with a reduction of the five-petal floribunda, won a series of prizes, established her name, and brought backers. She'd opened *Rosie's Tureen*, popularized the aphorism "the soup of the moment can transform a life," raised eight children, and upon her own grandmother's death retired to the family home.

On the two hundredth anniversary of the founding of Barsk, she was one of six mothers and aunts comprising the oldest generation in the house. Now, two generations later, she was the sole survivor of that cohort and had final word on all decisions within the house, though she'd rarely exercised it in the last tenyear, preferring to leave the routine tasks to a consortium of Pholo's great-aunts. Mostly Salaphora sat on the front porch of her enormous house and allowed her great-great-great-grandchildren to read to her, or else puttered in her design kitchen, tinkering with recipes for new soups.

Today word had spread throughout the house, a summons, politely worded but undeniable all the same. Pholo of course had been away, retrieving her prototype and arguing with Gavi and Bindle. A scattering of nieces and nephews had searched the boardways to find her and deliver the message. When one did, Pholo turned toward home. An audience with the head of house was the last thing she wanted after her insufferable exchanges with the man and woman who had her love and insisted they had her best interests at heart. She couldn't imagine life without Gavi and Bindle, though today she briefly wished she might.

Entering her home, Pholo paused only long enough to wash her hands and face in the guest powder room off the main foyer and then sped with all deliberate speed to the high balcony overlooking the yard where the children of the house were wont to play. There the old woman sat in a hammock chair, her once robust physique long since fallen in upon itself, leaving her wrinkled and wizened but no less formidable. She looked asleep, but Pholo knew better. Indeed it was rumored among her generation that the woman had dispensed with the need for sleep entirely.

"Granny Rosie," said Pholo, settling into a chair alongside the old woman. "You asked to see me?"

The woman stirred. "Did I? Oh, surely my memory is playing tricks on me. I remember asking after *someone* but that was back around breakfast and haven't I long since had my supper?"

So it was going to be like that, was it? "Please don't be cross with me, Granny Rosie. I was working. I came as soon as I heard you had need of me."

"Such a presumptuous child! Do you think I have needs? And if I did, do you truly believe you could fulfill them?"

"If I misspoke, I apologize, but surely you inferred my intention—"

"If? If you misspoke? Don't you know?"

Out of respect for her elder Pholo stifled an inclination to trumpet. She began again, lightly curling her trunk around the woman's hand. "Granny, you're having fun with me, aren't you? You know you mean the world to me and I'd never do anything to offend you. If you want to torment me with these games, well, that's your choice and I'll accept whatever judgment you've chosen for me. Only... hadn't there been some other reason you'd sent word for me in the first place?"

Salaphora raised her hand to her face, pressing the

tip of Pholo's trunk against her cheek. "Such a winning way you have, Pholo. Demure and cajoling and direct all in the span of a handful of breaths. Is it any wonder you're my favorite?"

"Granny Rosie, I have it on good authority that in the last tenday alone you've praised several dozen of my cousins and named them each as your favorite."

"Ah, Pholo, you are too clever by half. I blame your mother, she's the one who insisted on naming you that."

"What's wrong with my name?"

"Nothing at all, if you don't mind ambiguity. Your mother loved it. Why else choose a name for her only daughter that's as often borne by men as women among Lox. Since this house was founded there have been five born within its walls — three boys and two girls. When I was growing up, I had an uncle named Pholo. A brilliant man, though as I recall he came to a tragic end. A dish girl in my very first restaurant was named Pholo. And, about a tenyear before you came along, the cleverest woman to ever serve this island as mayor also had the name."

She gave Granny Rosie's hand a squeeze and said, "So you're saying that it's a name associated with smart people."

"Hrumph. Well, of course, you'd think so. But, as it turns out, that's part of why I wished to speak with you. Word has reached me — never you mind how or from whom — that your own cleverness is on a leaf's edge of getting you into more trouble than even I could pull you from."

"Was it Bindle? I can't believe she'd come to you and say—"

"What part of 'never you mind' lies beyond your comprehension, child?"

"Gavi? Did Gavi come to you? Does he think I'm a child to—"

"Be still! It wasn't Bindle, dearheart. Nor that physician you're so sweet on. If you must know — and it's clear I'll have no peace until you do — it was the fellow here from Telba, the young Eleph who's visiting your university for a term—"

"Scholar Ieri? He's far from young, he's twice my age. And he doesn't even know my name."

"Believe me, child, he knows quite a bit more than your name. Apparently he knows things that your academic advisors don't know. Things that if they did might have resulted in you being stripped of your stipend and your lab. Things that he has chosen to only hint at to me, in the hopes that I might dissuade you from whatever course he believes you to be on."

"Dissuade me? Why should he care to?"

"Well, as I understand it, he's of the opinion that you're bent on killing yourself in pursuit of theories he believes have no chance of being correct. He was quite adamant on that last point. No chance."

"That... that... buffoon! I spoke to him after one lecture, one! We discussed only the barest piece of my ideas, and he spins that into a judgment of my work? Calls me suicidal? Bothers my granny?"

"I'm sure he meant well, dear. And while I cannot pretend to have understood even half of the little this scholar knew and chose to share, I do know how headstrong you can be. When you get an idea into that mind of yours nothing and no one can change your course, not even yourself when you know you're wrong."

"Granny, please. That's not fair. That was just the one time, when I was nine, and Kimrel lied and Jefty might as well have lied and—"

"You buried your best friend up to her trunk in a mud pit in the Shadow Dwell and left her there overnight because she dared you that you wouldn't."

"I was nine!"

"Yes, well, now you're twenty-nine, and instead of a mud pit and a friend there's a traveling scholar who suspects you're going to kill yourself in a storm because you think it will prove some theory. Do I have the essentials right?"

Pholo's mouth hung open. She hadn't mentioned using extreme weather to Ieri, only shown him the math indicating the kind of vortices she'd deduced might be needed. How had he—

"This is what comes of thinking science is so important."

Oh no, not this argument again. For the last tenyear and more Pholo had argued for the primacy of science in her life, where the old woman had assured her it came in third, at best, well behind family and soup.

"Science is important. How could you think otherwise? You're the one who championed sending me to school in the first place after I tested above all the others in my class."

"Pay attention, you know better. I have never said science wasn't important, I said it wasn't *so* important. Especially compared to family. Honestly, for someone so smart I can't believe how confused your priorities are. Look around you, Pholo. All your relatives in this house, and others throughout this island and so many others. How can you not see what's more important?"

"Can we just agree to disagree? Like I disagree with Professor Ieri's views on my theories."

"He also said he thought your fundamental premises were all wrong" said Salaphora.

"He what? Granny Rosie, my premises are outstanding. My premises make my peers weep. My premises are beautiful and flawless and—"

"And wrong?"

"My Fundamental Premises Are Not Wrong!"

Salaphora flapped one ancient ear, an eloquent reminder that one did not shout in the house, let alone *at* the head of house. Not if one wished to remain part of the house. By way of rebuke all she said was "Well, dear, I'm sure you believe that, even if this Ieri fellow does not."

Pholo said nothing. There was nothing she could say. A renowned scholar had accurately extrapolated some conclusions based on a brief conversation about a small part of her work. He'd dismissed the possibility that she might be right, and instead of bringing his concerns directly to her like a proper colleague, he'd showed up at her home to tell her granny and make her fear that her great-great-granddaughter, inadvertently or perhaps intentionally, might take her own life.

She was done. It was over. She couldn't go against the wishes of Granny Rosie, no one could. The house overflowed with stories of her aunts and great-aunts wanting to pursue one life course or another, only to be overruled by Salaphora. And the worse still, in each and every instance, the old woman had been right and yet another child of the house had been saved from ruination. Because for Salaphora, family was everything.

"I'm going to ask you a question, Pholo. I want you to answer it honestly."

"Ma'am?"

"If I offered you this, would you give up this foolishness that you've set your mind on pursuing?" The old woman drew a small notebook from the folds of her robe.

"That's… that's your recipe book," said Pholo.

"It is."

Her mind croggled. "All your soups are in there. You've only let one person in the world look at those pages, and you swore her to secrecy when she took over your restaurant."

"That's true."

"And you're offering it to me? The recipes that made you famous? That caused dozens of scholars and artists and politicians to propose to you? That almost earned you an aleph?"

"This notebook, yes. It's yours, and all the things it can bring to you, if you'll step off the path you've chosen. Do we have a deal?"

"I… I… No, Granny Rosie. I'm sorry. What you're offering is a treasure I never dreamt might be mine, but… Please don't be angry, but no, I can't abandon my work. Please, please don't make me."

Nodding, Salaphora tapped the spine of the notebook lightly against Pholo's forehead. "Never you mind, child. I'm not angry. Truly, I'd have been disappointed if you'd accepted the offer."

"But… You said… What about what professor Ieri said?"

"Stuff that professor. All he knows is book learning. Mind you, that's important, but not as important as heart. If all you had was book learning you'd have snatched up my recipes and rushed off to make your own fortune and had a good life and grown fat and been happy and ended up in a big house surrounded by generations of adoring grandchildren. But maybe, maybe one day you'd have looked back at your life and asked what if you'd believed in yourself enough to follow your heart."

"Thank you, Granny Rosie. I hope I can do that, believe in myself enough, I mean."

"That's all right, my dear. There will be times when you falter. It's natural. When that happens, you need to remember only one thing."

"What's that?"

"I believe in you, too."

The Scholar

EVEN A HOUSE as vast as the one in which Pholo dwelled with its six generations of women and children, even such a place runs out of space. Much of it was given over to communal areas. There were several massive kitchens, each with an array of pantries and larders, cupboards brimming over with bowls and plates, drawers with cutlery and spoons, shelves and racks of seasonings and spices. There were parlors, large and small, some situated on the outermost layer of the house to accommodate visiting suitors and chaperones for the house's daughters. Others were hidden away deep within the house for more intimate conversations, meetings, and trysts. The house contained six separate libraries, one the size of the other five combined, with books and monographs and codices from all over Barsk. There were two nurseries, one at either end of the house, where infants and new mothers and the occasional wet nurse lived or slept, their occupants changing every season. There were tens of sleeping porches for the children, loosely sorted by gender and age, with rows upon rows of bunks and dressers and closets. The house boasted a hundred bathrooms, a number which once seemed wasteful but had long since proved inadequate to its population of residents and guests. And finally, there were the adults' bedrooms. Many of the more senior adults, Pholo's aunts and great-aunts and great-great-aunts, shared spaces, two or three women to a modest room, happy for the company and the routine and simple presence of family. Always family. Younger adults by tradition were granted the gift of privacy; each had a bedroom all their own as they established themselves in both the working and social worlds, building lives for themselves there on Kelprey.

Pholo's room was one of these last, or say rather it had been. She'd long since remodeled it, removing all traditional furnishings save for a modest cot and a single shelf for her clothing and a tub that lived under the cot for whatever other personal items she needed day to day. The rest of the space she had turned into her engineering lab. A massive workbench ran the length of the room, wall to wall, strewn with devices and components and models and prototypes and abandoned projects that would eventually be cannibalized and reborn in the next creation. An early version of her flying harness lay at one end of the table, this one bearing five stabilizing plates, before she had worked out the distribution flow to cut the need down to just three. The other end of the bench contained a range of objects, different ideas that had caught her fancy for a while before some fresh notion drove each in turn from her brain and she championed the new thing until it too faded. Midway upon the bench was the start of what she knew would be her defining work, the initial design of a transducing battery that, in theory, could harness the energy inherent in weather — primal and destructive, and by any definition and all common thinking, uncontrollable. From that first crude attempt with barely ten percent efficiency and enough waste energy that it had melted itself within seconds of activating — which just proved her point in terms of the amount of power she was tapping — to the flying harness she planned to test before the season was out, she had taken an impossibility and given it physical form.

Her lab was her sanctuary, more than any other adult's bedroom might be. In her mind it provided comfort and secrecy and autonomy, like the fantasy of a child's blanket fort. She had a lab at the university, a larger space than her bedroom, but she could not effectively lock it. Senior faculty might pop in without invitation, mentors and administrators, even custodial staff could gain entry at will. Students desperate to wheedle for a better grade knew they could track her down there, blithely interrupting her work and cluelessly inspiring her to seek ways to lower their grades. But at home, she could slip behind her door and steal hours free from distraction. She'd started simply, bringing home bits of gear and supplies four seasons ago. She'd bartered the construction of her workbench with a woodworking cousin whose daughter needed just a modicum of tutoring to shape her comprehension into something finer than she'd attain on her own, resulting in honors marks. A win-win that endeared her within her family.

In this small bedroom she'd traded personal comfort for the serenity that let her perfect those premises that visiting scholar Ieri had insisted must be flawed. The arrogance of the man, leaping to such dunderheaded conclusions on the basis of what... a moment's conversation with a junior scientist who'd foolishly sought the input from an academic luminary?

For most of the past tenday since her audience with

Granny Rosie, Pholo had been in her home lab. Every morning she'd emerged to one of the common dining rooms, pulled together the components of an enormous breakfast that would end up serving as nuncheon, dinner, and supper as well. With the bribe of a sweet she'd tasked one of the middle age children to carry a note to the university, canceling classes and/or office hours depending on the day. Any messages that might have arrived from either Gavi or Bindle were turned back by commiserating cousins and aunts who, certain she was making a mistake, nonetheless respected her desires and sent her lovers away with a hot bowl of soup and the encouragement that Pholo would come to her senses in time and that love, if true, could manage patience.

The rest of each of those days and nights, fueled by her anger at Ieri's presumption and buoyed up by Granny Rosie's faith, Pholo labored to perfect the flying harness.

And now it was done, fueled with the secondary battery that had charged those many days earlier with the unworn prototype. She lacked only the coming of the proper weather to power the main battery.

That morning Pholo'd bathed for the first time in longer than she could accurately recall, using so much time and hot water that a group of her cousins raided the bathroom and forcibly bundled her in towels and thrust her into a hallway, freeing up the room for others' use. Laughing, she'd dried and dressed and presented herself for a more social breakfast than she'd allowed herself of late. She disappointed the small pool of children who'd assembled anticipating that one among them would be given an errand and a treat, and made her way to the university and her office. She sent off a note first thing, and then spent the rest of the morning responding to the pile of inter-office memos and committee reports and grade sheets that she'd let slide for a tenday.

She ate a simple lunch of fruit and leaves at her desk. Midway through a student arrived, dropping off a reply to the morning's note. Half determined, half resigned, Pholo rose and left the simple building that contained the offices of junior faculty and made her way through the maze of paths to the heart of the university where, nestled amidst the majestic spaces given over to deans and provosts lay a handful of elegant buildings for visiting scholars. At some level Pholo had known she couldn't let things lie with Ieri. Now that she knew — knew with a certainty she felt in her bones — that her premises were not simply right but demonstrably so once the weather broke her way. She needed to set things straight. And perhaps at some level too, she hoped, he was having second thoughts, both about the assumptions he'd made on too little data, and the temerity of going to her great great-grandmother, as if Pholo were some cringing first year student who had been caught cheating on an exam. How else to explain his swift reply, inviting her to his offices that afternoon?

Pholo was greeted at the entrance by Ieri's secretary — imagine, his own secretary — and then moments later shown into an inner parlor where the scholar himself bade her sit in a sumptuous chair on the other side of a table of imported wood while he settled into a matching seat. Pholo bowed her head, determined to at least begin the encounter respectfully for all that she wanted to somehow conjure up a withering verbal attack and reduce him to jelly with her arguments and wit. Maybe later.

He offered her a hot beverage and made small talk for an uncomfortable span until in exasperation she interrupted some anecdote he was telling about the dissertation defense of one of a colleague's students that had gone horribly wrong.

"Speaking of colleagues, scholar Ieri, what kind of colleague is it that goes to one's grandmother?"

Ieri's ears fanned rapidly, as much an admission of wrongdoing as any confession though his words weren't quite as forthcoming. "A senior colleague seeking to assist a junior one. Please, Pholo, understand, I was concerned."

"Concerned? If you were concerned, why not come to me? Speak to me of the specifics, rather than bedevil my family with jargon they cannot follow while fueling their imaginations with dread."

He raised his trunk to halt her, then dropped it in acknowledgment. "You're right. Of course you're right. I handled that badly. I should have come to you directly. And for that I do apologize. And for any distress I've caused to your family. If there's something I can do to remedy that you have only to ask."

"Thank you, that's… that's appreciated, but—"

"But I'm not wrong."

Pholo blinked. "Excuse me?"

"I'm not wrong. The premises of your work are flawed and anything you build upon them is doomed to failure."

Pholo counted to eighteen. She lowered her gaze, took a deep breath and composed herself. Trunk down, ears back, hands folded in her lap, she felt almost calm. Then she lifted her eyes and saw the man across from her with an expression just the polite side of smugness. Did she have that wrong? Ieri was an Eleph, from the much more cosmopolitan island of Telba. Almost everyone on Kelprey was a Lox. With the exception of her therapist, every Fant that Pholo knew was a Lox. She had to entertain the possibility that her lack of experience with Elephs might be causing her to mistake his facial expression. Except, eyes were eyes, and Ieri's were laughing at her.

Her first inclination was to slap him, just rear back her trunk and let fly. Or better still, rise up from her seat, lunge across the table, and punch the smugness off his face, pummel the laughter out of those eyes. She did neither of these things and fell back into politeness as she'd been taught by her aunts.

"Most learned scholar," she said. "This is only our second meeting, and already it has exceeded the duration of the first. I have to wonder how you have become so thoroughly acquainted with my work to be in a position to evaluate its underlying premises, and why you would feel moved to do so." She smiled as she concluded, nodded once, and refreshed her beverage from the pot on the table.

"Do you truly believe you're the first bright-eyed postgrad to think about creating a transduction engine? Particularly here in the southwestern edge of your archipelago where the weather is, if anything, even more ferocious than most of Barsk?"

The world fell out from under her. In point of fact, she *had* believed her concept to be original. How could it not, or the world would be filled with people flying between islands. "You're not making any sense. If others have done it before, why haven't we seen the fruits of their efforts?"

The trace of a smirk formed at the edges of his mouth, though perhaps he thought better of it because he lifted up his cup and blocked her view of his expression. "Because it's flawed. It comes up every few years. I've had some of my best students come to me with thesis proposals on this topic, students who, frankly, based on conversations I've had with your colleagues here, possessed more talent and insight than you have shown."

She bristled "Scholar Ieri, is it your intention to offer me the benefit of your experience and factual knowledge or bestow your personal opinion in the guise of insults?"

Her own mother would have chided her for taking delight in making an elder sputter and spit into his own cup, but her mother wasn't here, and besides this buffoon had it coming. Flushed, he pulled a napkin from somewhere on his side of the table, wiping first his mouth and then his cup and finally the table.

"Pholo, as I told your great-grandmother—"

"My great-great-grandmother," she corrected.

He glared at her. No laughter lingering in his eyes. "As I told Salaphora, I'm trying to save your life."

"I'm fine."

"Only because you haven't reached the point where you've developed a prototype."

"I—"

He cut her off, his trunk reaching into her personal space, sweeping her words away. "Get your ego in check, Pholo. I've seen the results with my own eyes on two occasions, promising scholars whose careers ended because they ignored advice, torn apart by their own hubris."

"If you'd just come to my lab, not the one here, the one I work out of at home—"

He leapt to his feet, trumpeting his dismay. "You've been working on this from your family home? Are you completely irresponsible? Even if you care nothing for your own well being, how could you threaten the safety of your household by trying to control the weather from inside your home?"

"Excuse me? The weather?"

Ieri came around the table and loomed over her. "Do not play dumb with me, Pholo. Are you some kind of idiot savant then? Gifted in science but utterly devoid of common sense? Are you or are you not working on a transduction engine capable of harnessing the weather?"

"Yes. Yes, but—"

He stomped. "It cannot be done. The forces involved are too vast. You can no more sample a portion of a storm and control the weather than you can go down to the beach, wrap your arms in a wave and claim you have hold of the ocean."

Pholo blinked and blinked again. "You think I'm trying to control the weather?"

"Give it up. The systems involved span the planet. I've seen the simulations, I understand why you'd pursue it. In the miniature of a model it looks like it should work, in theory, but the practice is something else entirely. The energies unleashed in even the most basic of first attempts invariably destroy the apparatus. In attempting to control the weather all anyone has managed to do was bring a portion of it to them, concentrate it in a fraction of the space it requires, and expose themselves to devastation."

He'd misunderstood. He must think her an imbecile. Control the weather? Well, sure, that might be the first, most obvious goal in creating the means to transduce the power of a storm into something useful and controlled. But he was right, the power was too vast to be controlled. She'd seen that in her first equations, you'd have to be the island's idiot not to see it. It would take an engine bigger than any ten islands to accomplish that, and then what would you do with the resulting energy, blow up a moon?

But he hadn't looked further, none of them had. They'd let the logic of impossibility stop them from asking the next question, not to control weather but to harness a tiny fraction of it, bleed off an infinitesimal portion that would still yield enormous energy, store it and redirect it in a symmetrical way that didn't blow you up for the effort.

She stood, hid the grin that wanted to refute him, the laughter she longed to fling in his face. Call her imbecile and idiot? This traveling scholar who had leapt to assumptions on little knowledge? She'd relish going beyond his narrow-minded misunderstanding and flying rings around him.

Pholo didn't let any of that show. Instead she met

his eyes and made him a promise. "Thank you, Scholar Ieri. I had not considered the matter in quite that way. Certainly I have no desire to bring harm to either myself or my family. You have my word, I will abandon any attempt to control the weather. It's a foolish undertaking."

He regarded her in silence, nodding after a moment. "I am sorry if I seem harsh. It's not foolish to want to understand Nature's powers. We all find inspiration in such pursuits. But the wise researcher knows his limits. You might as well attempt to drink the rain."

"That really puts it in perspective," she replied.

"Oh? How so?"

"Well… think how much control one would need to have over the weather to even think of drinking up all the rain."

He grinned at her, a genuine expression it seemed, and his ears relaxed at her weak joke. "Good luck to you, Pholo. I know this may seem like a defeat, having to abandon what you've obviously put a great deal of effort into, but you will go on to do great things."

"You think so?"

He shrugged, some thought's passing changing his assessment of her. "I told you I've seen other students go down this path? All of them were brilliant. You'd never have reached this point if you were not similarly gifted. All the more reason for me to save you from yourself."

"Um… thank you?"

"You have much to offer the world, Pholo. Go find out what form that's going to take."

Dismissed, she left the parlor, left the building, left the campus. She wandered the boardways of Kelprey's

Civilized Wood, her heart light, her spirit free, schooling her mind to patience for the turning of the seasons. Soon, so very soon, she would fly.

The Heart

PHOLO SENT messages to both Gavi and Bindle, invitations to meet up with them separately. Bindle had left Kelprey during the days of silence, not because of Pholo but to fill in at a gig on Phran for another poet who had injured herself in a freak accident. Gavi likewise proved to be unavailable, quarantined after exposure to a patient from the other archipelago who had come in contact with several health workers who were now all showing the same symptoms. The domina at his rooming house, which was also the home for a couple of the other infected, assured her that they were all expected to make a full recovery once the virus ran its course.

With a glad heart she gathered flowers and created a bouquet that she left on Granny Rosie's balcony, with a short note to let her know the matter with the visiting scholar had been resolved. And then, just to put a bow on it, she'd stopped in to beg a favor of the aunt who supervised the house's commercial kitchen, arranging for a pot made from Salaphora's most famous recipe to be delivered to that same scholar, a token that he'd interpret as contrition and appreciation. Buffoon. But it was like her great great-grandmother always said, the soup of the moment could transform a life.

Since finishing her degree program two years earlier, Pholo had been under a lot of pressure. The university on Kelprey was a shadow of the academic opportunities on distant Zlorka, but even so the competition among the junior faculty had been a constant source of stress since her first tenday there. Midway through her first season, she'd felt more overwhelmed than back when she was a graduate student. Her lectures had become erratic, her Dean had stopped by her office seeking a casual conversation — rather than a formal inquiry — about a rumor that she'd yelled at some of her students and threatened to fail them preemptively if they didn't "cease being stupid dunderheads with cabbages instead of brains." In return for this kindness, Pholo had adopted a defensive posture, snapped at the Dean, and insisted that *dunderheads* was a grossly generous insult given the students involved. That had earned her a provisional red mark. Another would bring her before the faculty senate and the very real possibility of termination. A third would ensure not only her departure but pretty much guarantee that no university on any island would take her on for even the most unctuous of courses. Worse still, no funding sources would look at her grant proposals.

Not surprisingly, this only added to her stress and by the end of the second season she'd lost a disturbing amount of weight and started having sleep issues. The lack of sleep brought a malaise that made it nearly impossible for her to do the mental work required of her, which in turn punched up her paranoia. She'd begun to suspect that Gavi, that sweet boy who doted on her, was actually sleeping with one of her cousins and only pretending to be in love with Pholo as a means of getting into her house. And Bindle, gentle Bindle, was also conniving to somehow steal Granny Rosie's recipes. Her life had been falling apart, but in a rare moment of clarity she let Gavi convince her to seek out a therapist who'd been a classmate from his own school days.

And so she'd met Maefis, her first Eleph.

Maefis saw her clients in a back room of a salad bar restaurant on the edge of the university district, so the place had a constant customer flow of both students and faculty. She'd worked out some arrangement with the owner to provide a free lunch for each of her clients, which more often than not resulted in her clients coming back for other meals. That was Maefis, unconventional and never what you expected. She actually had tested positive for the Speaker's gift, but never bothered to develop the talent to summon the dead, insisting that the living were far more interesting.

From her very first appointment, Maefis had helped Pholo with assorted cognitive therapies to reframe the stressful aspects of her situation, focusing her efforts on those things she could affect and absolving her of others that existed independently of anything she might say or do. She didn't judge. She vetted any of Pholo's life choices, so long as they were deliberate choices and not passive acceptances of others' decisions. Much of it was the same kind of advice that her aunts had offered, but of course it's easier to hear a stranger than a family member. Pholo began to recover after her third session and had completely regained her equilibrium by the tenth. The Dean generously removed the red mark from her record, and her student evaluations at the end of her third season were among the finest of any of the junior faculty. Her visits to Maefis decreased in frequency, trailing off to an occasional follow-up just to check in.

She'd been overdue for just such a follow-up for more than a tenday, putting it off while she worked to complete her prototype. But the lull created by her wait for the weather to turn, as well as her barely suppressed glee at Ieri's cluelessness as to her real project, had her thinking that now was a good time for a visit.

Her therapist met her in line at the restaurant. Both prepared massive bowls of salad and instead of taking a table carried their meals down the hall to Maefis's office. They sat on adjacent sides of her desk and took up the challenge of their meal. Around a mouthful of greens, Maefis asked, "So tell me what's going on," and Pholo did, glossing over the details of her project but otherwise leaving nothing unsaid.

"So, you've been under some extra stress again, but nothing that you can't handle. But the way things keep piling up for you, with that scholar, and your project, are you losing ground in other areas? What about your love life? How are things with Bindle, with Gavi?"

"They're part of the stress. They don't support my project."

"I can see how that could be a problem. Any chance you're over-personalizing that?"

"Meaning what, exactly?"

"You said they didn't support your project. Are you making that mean they don't support you?"

Pholo raised her trunk to object and stopped. Was that what she was doing? "I know they love me. They both do."

"Right, that's what your head knows. Does your heart know that too?"

"Bindle is my best and oldest friend. Always has

been, always will be. And Gavi, he… we… we're going to spend our lives together."

"Fair enough. But let me ask what your mother would ask in response. If that's true, then why haven't you bonded? Do you have something against marriage?"

"No, it's not like that. We plan on getting married. But not yet. I'm not ready to have children!"

"Lots of married couples manage not to have children. Just because bonding is a prerequisite doesn't mean you'll conceive the first time you're intimate afterwards."

Pholo flushed, fanning her ears rapidly to dissipate the sudden heat she felt. "We… we have a lot of sex. I'm not ready to settle down into motherhood and I don't want to treat the possibility like a game of chance."

"Got it. Okay, so, there's that, too, contributing to your current state. Hmm."

"What?"

"Well, all in all, what you've told me suggests that you're coming up to a choice point."

"You've never used that term before," said Pholo. "What does it mean?"

Maefis laughed and her trunk tip lightly rubbed her frontal lobes, that prominent feature of all Elephs. "I don't believe in a lot of jargon. It means a point in your life where you need to make a choice. There are decisions that are coming due. Avoiding them is just going to keep backing you up."

"You're right. I know you're right. But I guess I'm having trouble seeing the big picture. I'm so caught up in all the minutia."

Pushing her plate aside, Maefis pulled a rounded

deck of cards from a shelf. "That's something I can help with."

Pholo frowned at her. "Are you a fortune teller now? Are you going to read my cards?"

"Nothing of the kind. You're going to do all the reading."

"I'm a scientist. I don't believe in that kind of mysticism. Do you?"

Her therapist shrugged. "What I believe isn't important. And in this instance, what you believe doesn't matter so much either. The results will speak for themselves."

"I don't understand."

"Do you know what a *projective test* is?"

Pholo shook her head and flapped her ears.

"It's really quite simple. I show you an ambiguous image, and I ask you what it means. In turn, your unconscious mind offers up answers, projecting meaning onto the thing you see."

"So, nothing psychic?"

"For a scientist like you? I wouldn't dream of it. Nothing but psychology."

Pholo smirked. "I have quite a few colleagues who would bristle at implying that psychology is a science."

"Good thing they're not here. Now, shuffle those cards and then deal out six in a spread in front of you from right to left, face down."

"Why six?"

"The number isn't important. I could just have easily picked nine, but I don't think we need it. Now, I'm going to assign a context to each and you'll fill in the details as you reveal each card. Let's call them the Past, the Near

Past, the Present, the Obstacle, the Near Future, and the Future. When you're ready, turn over the first card."

Pholo shuffled, dealt. She turned over the first card, revealing an image of mud and streams, rocks and the roots of the mighty meta-trees that their forest home was built on. A small frame at the bottom of the image bore the name of the card. She read it even as Maefis said it aloud.

"'The Shadow Dwell,' what does that mean for you?"

"It's the basis of everything we've built on Kelprey. The foundation established by our ancestors."

"Good. Next card."

"Wait, is that what the card really means?"

"It means what you choose it to mean. Projective test, remember? But don't overthink it. Just react. Your unconscious will fill in the rest. Now, turn over the second card."

She did so. Row upon row of singing children looked up at her.

"That's the Chorus," said Maefis. "Can you tell me what's going on in that card?"

"They're kids."

"And?"

"They're... singing? Putting on a performance, maybe in a public park, maybe in the parlor of a large home."

"What else?"

"I don't know. There's an audience, probably their loved ones. I mean, they look happy, their singing isn't a chore or a burden. They like what they're doing, and they like doing it for their family. It's the kind of thing you remember when you look back on your childhood, you know? It doesn't happen every day, maybe not even often. Eventually you grow up and have to become an adult. Fun as singing is, it's not going to sustain you. But it's a sweet memory."

"Next card."

Pholo turned over a card showing a cornucopia overflowing with all sorts of fruits and nuts, a veritable feast.

"That one's called the Harvest," said Maefis. "What does that mean for you?"

"Um, bounty? Plenty for all. Freedom from want?"

"Good enough. fourth card. Don't hesitate."

Pholo frowned. Hesitate? Why would she hesitate? She flipped the card and gasped. The image was of a malformed newborn. An Abomination.

"What's that one represent to you?"

"It's a broken infant," she said. "Dead, or dying."

Maefis waggled her trunk. "I didn't ask what the image was of. What do you think of when you see it? What does it represent?"

"Abominations only happen when children are born without bonding. They're supposed to be impossible. I'd have to say it represents disorder. Chaos. A breakdown of the natural flow of things A... a wrongness."

"Fair enough. An interesting place to put such a card."

"What do you mean?"

"Fourth card in this spread represents the story you tell yourself about what's holding you back or getting in your way. Don't worry about that just now. Go forward."

The nubs of Pholo's trunk gripped the edge of the

deck and flipped the next card over, revealing a vast expanse of dark clouds.

Maefis named it. "The Wind."

Pholo froze.

"Talk to me. Is that significant for you? What does the Wind mean for you?"

"Significant? What? No, it's just a card. Just the wind."

"Which means?"

"It could mean anything to anybody."

"It's your card, yours is the only opinion that matters."

"It's… uncertain. I mean, which way is the wind blowing? Are all those dark clouds coming towards me or away? It could be showing a storm coming in or one blowing out to sea. Something's happening, but it could be either extreme."

"But it is extreme?"

"Do you not see those clouds?"

Maefis smiled. "I do indeed. Last card."

She turned it over. The last card was black with a tiny scattering of pinpricks of white.

"The Universe," said Pholo.

"Yep. Your universe."

"Not really, the card is a lie."

"Is it? How so?"

"You can't see space from Barsk. The cloud cover never breaks that much. You'd have to be standing on the other side of the atmosphere to have a view like that."

"Are you saying that the only things that are real are the ones you can see?"

"Of course not. The universe is out there, it's real, it's ours. But it's beyond our daily lives. It's a reminder that we're both a part of something so much bigger than any of us, and also apart from who we are. It's possibilities that we may never even notice."

Maefis took up the six cards, shuffled them back into the deck, squared them with a thump against the table, and put them away. "Great. You did really well."

"What are you talking about?"

"We're done. That's your spread."

Pholo shook her head again. "I don't understand."

"That's because you're a very literal person, and this is heavily figurative. The spread is a metaphor supplied by your unconscious. Take some time to reflect on the images and what you said they mean. The Shadow Dwell was your past. You described it as foundational. Your near past was the Chorus, and you called that a sweet memory of family, but also something that cannot sustain you through adulthood. The third card, the Harvest, is your present. Bountiful, prosperous. The next, the Abomination, that's the obstacle before you. You're struggling with something that some might consider fundamentally wrong. Your fifth card, the Wind, your near future, is powerful, but uncertain. And the last was the Universe, possibilities, if only we could see them."

Pholo fanned her ears and pushed back in her chair. "I thought you said you weren't a mystic?"

"I'm a therapist. All I did was name the cards you dealt. You told me the stories of each one. And this works because they're your stories. How could they be otherwise? What just happened is I distracted your conscious awareness for a few moments so your unconscious mind could tell you what it's been thinking about. You've just had a chat with yourself, I just happened to be here while you did it. You covered six essential topics: what's important, where you're coming from, where you are, what's in your way, what lies before you, and where you hope to go."

"How did you know those cards would come up?"

Maefis shrugged. "I didn't. It doesn't matter. Pholo, it's a metaphor. You'd have managed to tell yourself the same story if you'd dealt yourself different cards like the Lovers or the Grandmother or the World."

"I... I've got a lot to think about."

"Great," said Maefis. "Come back when you've had a chance to work out what it all means. And when you do, don't forget to bring some of your family's soup."

Pholo smiled, picking up the empty salad bowls and carrying them to drop off in the restaurant on her way out.

The Wind

THE SEASON of dark came to its inevitable end, just as the season of mist had before it. There is always rain on Barsk, but during dark even as the rain falls the clouds grow denser, elementally gravid. That meteorological water breaks in the season of storm and the weather achieves its most violent state. Thunder and lightning are nearly constant. Waterspouts occur daily, often in the spaces between islands, and cyclones are a constant danger.

Never had Pholo been so excited to hear the weather forecast discussed over breakfast.

On the third day of storm she again tasked one of her younger cousins to deliver messages to both Gavi and Bindle. Both were simple and to the point:

TODAY IS THE DAY.
MEET ME AT OUR FAVORITE BEACH
AT DUSK TO CELEBRATE.

As her messenger sped off she packed up her equipment and began to climb the series of ramps and staircases and ultimately ladders that took her to the top of the forest's canopy where a bare platform lay exposed to the violent weather that gave the season its name.

She climbed into a silk one-piece that was sodden before she had it halfway on, then tucked her ears back and down so she could pull the hood over her head. A matching pair of silk panes billowed on either side along the lines from her wrists to her ankles, a little extra help to catch the wind and keep her aloft and lessen the drain on her battery. She added gloves, gripping socks, and heavy polarizing goggles. Last she pulled on her flight harness, adjusted the uncharged main battery and the more limited test battery that she'd shown to her lovers and which had precipitated so much stress. Likely neither of her lovers would recognize her as she now stood, dressed in her gear.

Pholo recalled the spread of cards from days earlier, what Maefis had called a projective test. The third card, the Harvest, represented her present. Abundance. This was her moment. She stood tall, arms and legs spread wide. She felt the wind pull at her clothing and with her trunk slapped the activation switch at the center of her chest. The harness buzzed as power flowed through it and Pholo launched herself into the air.

The wind caught her before she'd jumped an ear's span above the platform. Her harness grabbed at the air and pulled her higher. With rain pummeling her, lightning flashing all around and the air vibrating with thunder, she flew up… up… up… into the rain, closer to the ever present ceiling of clouds. At twice the height of her forest home a warning light flashed in the heads-up display of her goggles. Even so brief a flight as that had already burned through five percent of her battery. She needed to find a storm soon, or she wouldn't be able to charge the larger battery, at which point she'd become nothing more than flotsam in the air, and that only briefly, until she succumbed to gravity and fell to earth.

She climbed higher into the sky. Kelprey dwindled beneath her, barely visible through the curtains of rain. Neighboring islands came into dim view as well. And there, further south than her home, a distortion in the air, a smudge that blurred a tiny piece of rainy plane, suggesting the existence of a cyclone. Pholo pulled her arms and legs in, the silk wings had provided lift but would only create drag now. She hurtled like a bolt toward the storm, a counter in her goggles ticking off her shrinking power level. This high up the air was thinner, harder to breathe, and the rain barely warmer than ice. As she neared the halfway point the storm was still far ahead of her. She might not reach it, might not charge the new battery. If she turned back now, she could land safely, charge the smaller battery as she had before and live to fly another day. But no, today, this moment, was her present. She would reap her harvest and claim her future. That fourth card, the Wind, with all its uncertainty and power called to her. She let the counter tick down. It passed the midway point, she was committed.

She was down to twenty percent when she reached the edge of the cyclone. The fury of the winds hurled the rain at her with such velocity that every second a thousand icy needles slammed into her. The silk held, but if she survived, no, when she survived, she'd be bruised head to toe. Rather than fight the vortex she followed its direction, like swimming with a tide, if that tide spun sunwise and had the strength to strip a forest bare. Pholo tucked her chin to her chest and pulled her body into as small a ball as possible, protecting the more sensitive components of her device including the new uncharged transducing battery. She instructed her flight harness to edge ever inward. She moved as a part of the storm's rotation even as it pulled her along its course, like a planet both rotating on its axis and revolving around its star. Pholo doubted space could possibly be as freezing as this storm. Still, bit by bit, she pierced its layers until with only four percentage points of power — already within the plus or minus error range — she tumbled into the calm air of the cyclone's eye.

A moment to catch her breath; that was all she allowed herself. Now she would prove her theory and design or fail utterly. Live or die.

Her flight harness was a marvel, undeniably so, converting the stored power of the weather into a controlled kinetic release, as if she owned a piece of the wind and could command it to carry her whither she wished. But at its heart, it was her transducing battery that made it all possible. The prototype had worked well enough, a proof of concept, but the method she'd employed, tapping the winds at the top of the forest, had taken two full tendays and drenched the gear in lethal levels of radiation as a byproduct. Here in the center of a cyclone she expected the process to be five to six orders of magnitude swifter. Assuming it worked.

Pholo unfolded from a ball, bidding her harness to hold her upright as if she stood in the air, arms akimbo. The moment had come. She activated the battery on its lowest setting, easing into the transduction.

Nothing happened. All around her the vortex spun, the storm raged and continued drifting south. Her harness nudged her forward, keeping her in the center of the calm. Wait, it was hard to judge, but something was changing, the cyclone had slowed, barely. She called up another gauge in her goggles' display above the one for the secondary battery which now showed barely two percent. Yes, the main battery had begun to charge, six percent, already surpassing the reading of the other, despite its much larger capacity.

And then she began to fall.

Pholo shrieked. That two percent reading had been a lie. The smaller battery was out of power and her harness could no longer hold her aloft. She plunged through the calm air, striking the inner edge of the storm and being swept trunk over tail into the howling vortex. Panicking, she grasped at habit. The repetition of days spent drilling saved her as the nubs of her trunk switched the power flow from the useless battery to the little energy available in the main one. She stabilized at once but she used up most of the small reserve fighting her way back to the eye. Again the meter began to tick upward, but if something else went wrong she doubted she'd survive to get a third chance.

"This is my moment," she told herself again. "Abundance!" She opened the transducing battery to its highest setting. The gauge on her heads-up display climbed, ten percent, twenty, fifty-five, ninety. And as simply as blowing out a candle flame she stopped being at the center of a cyclone. The storm simply unwound and vanished, its elemental power transduced and stored.

"Premises," she shouted into the ordinary rain. "Premises, Scholar Ieri!"

She extended her arms and legs and with her nubs instructed the flight harness to reorient back toward her home of Kelprey. She flew north, accompanied by the thunder and lightning normal to the season, descending slightly as she went, deliriously happy with herself despite the soaking rain. With gravity on her side, flying took very little power. Technically, she was still falling, but in a controlled, mostly deliberately lateral way. Increasing altitude took energy, but this, this she could do all day.

Pholo had plenty of time before dusk. She could circle Kelprey a couple times before Gavi and Bindle reached the beach, and then she'd fly a few rings around them, a loop or two, maybe a barrel roll before she landed to bask in their astonishment.

Such a sweet dream, and she'd surely earned it. Now that it was behind her, she could admit to the madness of what she'd done, how she'd risked everything. What would Maefis say about her recklessness, about the dangers of failure? But she hadn't failed. Now she would return triumphant, run some test flights, document her analyses, and present her results to the university where that buffoon Ieri would admit he'd been wrong wrong wrong, and the Dean would grant her tenure, and she and Gavi could marry and life would be perfect.

All of that might have come to pass, if not for the lightning. A bolt struck her flight harness as she neared her island, before she could begin her first victory lap around it, low enough to be seen by anyone on its beaches as she plummeted toward the treeline. The operating system on her flight harness locked up and shut down. Like a part of the storm, she fell from the sky.

The Forest

PHOLO STRUCK THE CANOPY. Hard. Consciousness was the first casualty, which eliminated the trauma of witnessing what came next. Branches broke some of her fall and broke her as well, or at least one arm. The struts of her flight harness took the brunt of that first, worst impact, bending and ultimately splintering. Its three stabilizing plates shattered, bits of enamel and slender circuitry scattering into the air all around. Her slick silk one-piece spared her thousands of lacerations and even the rain aided her, creating a thin cushion as she burst through the foliage.

She tumbled and crashed through the green of her island, breaking through to a commercial neighborhood, the shops recently closed and its minor boardway deserted. She lay in a heap, the frame of her harness mangled, its principal components broken or simply gone. Her goggles had cracked. Her one-piece had shredded in several places starting at the hood, and one ear had come free only to be scratched and cut, bleeding in several places. A long patch of skin had torn open on her left arm where one end of her broken ulna showed through. Less than a fifth of the framework of the flight harness remained, and only a small piece of one of the stabilization plates. Miraculously, the transducing battery was still strapped across her abdomen, though its connections to the rest of the suit had been severed. Per its internal program, it ran an independent self check and produced a faint buzz of readiness, so that was good.

Time passed and perhaps her body decided the threat and chaos had ended and it was time to awaken. Her eyelids fluttered and she knew she was alive because she'd never felt such agony before. The slightest movement increased the pain so she lay still, focusing first on just breathing and slowing the beating of her heart while she began to assess her situation.

"Okay, pros and cons," she said, pleased that her voice was working. "Pros: I'm alive. And I'm out of the rain. And… okay, maybe I'll find some others in a bit. Um… Cons: I'm hurt, not sure how bad. And I think I totaled my gear. And there's no one around to help me so whatever else needs to happen now, I'm going to need to manage myself." Grimacing, she rolled to her right side and tried to sit up. Her left arm came around and she saw blood and bone. "And there's the whatever, a compound fracture. Huh. Go figure. So… maybe I'm in shock, too? Probably not thinking too clearly. Probably anything I come up with is suspect."

Pholo managed to get to her knees, propping herself up on her right hand. She pushed with her trunk and slowly got to her feet, left arm dangling. She staggered to the side of the boardway and would have fallen but caught herself against the wall of a sweet shop. She leaned there awhile, consciousness dancing in and out. The pain throbbed with the same rhythm as the pounding of her heart. She stared in through the shop window at the display of colorful confections and smiled. She knew this place. Bindle had brought her here on a date once and they'd gone on to a picnic where they'd fed each other candied grasses. It was a short stroll to the apartment Bindle used when she was on

Kelprey. That clicked.

"I know where I am. I just need to get to Bindle's and I'll be fine. That's doable, right? 'course it is."

Shoving off from the sweet shop she staggered from storefront to storefront until she reached the side ramp leading down to the residential level below. It looked impossibly steep though she knew it was really a gentle grade, polished wood that children could race down with impunity.

"You can do this, 'lo," she told herself. "Baby steps. Gravity's on your side. Ha, cuz that's never bitten you in the ass."

Facing the wall on the right so she could grasp at it with both her trunk and one working hand she sidestepped her way down, focusing on the space in front of her, on the routine task of extending her left foot a tiny bit, stopping, sliding her right foot down until it hit her left, stopping, and then over again. The process established, she lost herself in the repetition until after an infinite number of cycles the floor leveled. She'd reached the end of the ramp.

She was on a cul-de-sac of bachelor apartments. Bindle, the rebel poet lived here three out of five seasons. It was uncommon, scandalous to some minds, though her male neighbors, young and old, counted themselves fortunate to have her in their midst and often invited her to their weekly drinking outings. Quiet Bindle could be wild Bindle. Pholo had gone along on one of the binges and seen her lover match the men cup for cup, laughing and singing. In the end, Bindle had stood upon the table and performed an impromptu poem that was equal parts awe-inspiring and pornographic. The men had cheered. Bindle had saluted them with a final cup, then taken Pholo's hand and led her back to the apartment and they'd made love and woken up with terrible hangovers.

"Not far now," she said to herself, stumbling across the impossibly long gaps between apartments, dragging herself along their doorways until reaching the fifth one. She wanted to pound on it but only managed a weak knock.

It was the wrong door in any case.

"Please be home. Please be home."

Days seemed to pass and her legs didn't want to hold her up any more. That was fine, the doorway looked comfy. She slumped and slid and collapsed. Moments after her knock the door opened and a man stared down, gasping at the sight of her.

"I know you," he said. "You're Bindle's friend. The soup girl. What's done this to you? You look like hell."

Pholo swam up though the Shadow Dwell of her mind to full awareness. "You don't look too good either, Bindle. You look like an old man."

The elder in question glanced both ways from his door and then stooped and lifted Pholo as gingerly as he could.

"Ima gonna get you settled inside, put a couple blankets on you, and then fetch Bindle. It'll be all right, don't you worry."

"I'm not worried, Bindle."

"My name's Ostwick."

"Nyah," said Pholo. "You're my sweet Bindle girl." Confident of her company, she surrendered to unconsciousness again.

* * *

When she woke again the real Bindle was there, gently tending her wounds. She still lay on Ostwick's couch but her silk one-piece had been further reduced to tatters cutting it off her. Someone had wrapped her naked body in warm blankets. Gavi was there too, and he had done something to her left arm and plugged an intravenous drip of something or other into her right one. She felt wonderful and let her eyes close again.

"She's going to be fine," he said. "She's taken quite a beating, but other than the broken arm everything else is pretty superficial. With rest and fluids she'll be back on her feet in a tenday. The drip should keep the pain away, but she's not going to be giving any lectures at the university while she's on it."

"She can stay on my couch if need be," said Ostwick, his voice coming from the far side of the room, sounding uncomfortable despite his spoken generosity.

"There's no need," said Bindle. "Easy enough to get her a few doors down to my place, that is if she can be moved. Gav?"

"I think between us we can carry her well enough. But I'd say wait until she's awake and knows what we're doing rather than risk her coming to in the middle and flailing about."

"I am awake," said Pholo, opening her eyes. "Why aren't we on the beach?"

"Imma gonna take a walk," said Ostwick. "Just up a ways to the pub. Have a cup and give you folks some privacy for a spell." Without waiting for a response he let himself out his own door and shut it behind him.

"We were," said Gavi. "We both showed up at dusk, like your notes said. We were scared and pissed and then you didn't come. And we went to your house but your family said you weren't there either and didn't know where you were. So we left. I had rounds and Bindle went home."

"And a good thing I did," added Bindle. "Ostwick fetched me after you showed up on his doorstep, and then he went and fetched Gavi. You're a mess, 'lo. What happened? What did you do?"

"I flew," she said, smiling for more than the golden rain flowing through her veins. "I flew into the heart of a storm. And I ate it whole."

"You're saying it worked?" Bindle glanced at Gavi, both their faces full of doubt.

"Oh yeah. More than worked. Excelled. It was awesome."

"You don't look awesome," said Gavi. "And if this is excelling, I don't want to see failure."

"No, no, this," she tried to lift her arms and shrug but they stayed put there at her sides. Her trunk waved lazily. "This was after. This was the lightning."

"Lightning? You were struck by lightning?" Gavi gasped.

"Yeah… pretty much fried… everything. Stopped me cold. Except, well, stopping in mid-air means falling. But before that, I was flying. I wish you could have seen it, it was glorious. Can't wait to do it again."

"Again?" Bindle frowned. "What do you mean again?"

"You're not in any shape to do anything," said Gavi.

"A tenday. You said I'd be fine."

"Your gear's destroyed. The harness frame is a twisted wreck."

"I can twist it back."

"And the stabilizer plates? Aren't there supposed to be three? You only had a fragment of one on you."

"I can make new ones."

"And your goggles are cracked, they—"

"None of that matters," said Pholo. "Yeah, all of that is so much junk, but it's replaceable junk. The one part that matters, the densest and irreplaceable piece, that came through just fine."

"What are you talking about?" said Gavi.

"The battery. I wore it on my chest. I curled tight when I crashed, not just to protect myself, but to safeguard it. It came through just fine, and it's barely a fraction off fully charged."

The World

THE MAJORITY of Pholo's bruises, those acquired from the force of the cyclone's rain, healed within a tenday. Those earned from crashing through the canopy, though much fewer in number, also went deeper and required more time before she could manage any appreciable movement without pain.

The family home had a solarium, a room filled with daylight trickling down through the forest by means of an elaborate collection of shafts and vents, mirrors and lenses. Pholo convalesced in that space, attended by an endless rotation of doting aunts and great-aunts who withheld voicing any judgment but sucked the tips of their trunks in their mouths every time they left her presence, making faint *tsk tsk* sounds. More approving, though probably as a result of a morbid fascination with the ever changing mottling of her skin as she healed, were the gaggle of nieces and nephews who waited on her every whim or need. And every afternoon, usually while she was asleep, Granny Rosie passed through and left a fresh bowl of soup.

It wasn't a bad arrangement for the first tenday. Her body needed rest more than her mind needed to race ahead to solve the mundane matters of securing the materials to rebuild her flight harness. Into the second tenday though, against the insistence of those same aunts, a quartet made up of older, bigger children half carried her back to her lab. She didn't have the strength yet to work very long, but she also didn't have the strength to not work at all. The nieces and nephews were given new tasks. They brought her tools, took detailed lists of raw materials to the handful of manufacturers on Kelprey who could provide the pieces she needed, or failing that, the materials from which she could build things to create the pieces she needed. Other children let themselves into her lab at the university, liberating a few key instruments she needed back at home.

Her department head at the university had granted her a medical furlough without asking any questions, possibly fearing that answers might expose some liability. Such self-serving discretion suited Pholo just fine. An even more junior faculty member had stopped by two days into her recovery. She'd left with the details of Pholo's courses' syllabi, the key to an upcoming exam, and a gleam in her eye suggesting she intended to make the most of the opportunity handed to her. Pholo didn't care, didn't feel threatened. Her mind was already far ahead down a different path.

She recalled the final three cards Maefis had shown her, the ones representing obstacles and near and more distant futures. The obstacle card had been the Abomination, a thing unnatural and wrong. Pholo refused to believe that applied to her discovery for flight, but if Gavi was an indication there would be plenty of people who would react to it that way. Fine, she'd just have to come up with a way to win them over despite their prejudice.

Pholo grinned. Maefis had been right. She didn't pretend to understand all that talk about her unconscious sorting through things, but the cards had allowed Pholo to better appreciate what she was trying to accomplish and how to frame the problems she needed to resolve. And the future she imagined for herself, whether the immediate uncertainty personified by the Wind or the broader possibilities of the Universe, that future was hers to manifest and shape.

After a full pair of tendays the throbbing in her arm stopped being a distraction, the worst of her lacerations had healed, and she was able to forego the appetite suppression and constipation of her pain meds and embrace a full meal instead of the trunkfuls of nuts that had sustained her. Gavi, who had been stopping in at least once a day to check up on her, took her away that night. He'd made reservations at a restaurant she knew full well he could not afford, plying her with succulent leaves, a compote of fruit not found on any island within a day's sailing, and a bottle of a refreshing mist wine that stopped on the right side of being too sweet.

There was a shyness to him that night, something she'd not seen since their days in gymnasium together. He'd excelled at his advanced studies, and the growing knowledge and skills had filled him with confidence that went beyond just his abilities as a surgeon, paying dividends in every aspect of his life. From their first early fumblings in stolen moments together he had prospered into a talented and generous lover, the perfect partner for her, really, and quite beloved by her entire family who were growing impatient for them to bond and get on with their lives.

Her mind danced to that aspect of her future as they strolled the boardways in the evening air. Somehow, they wound their way from the restaurant back to

Gavi's rooming house, through the charming courtyard and ultimately into his bed. Under the guise of reviewing her recent injuries he kissed and stroked every inch of her body, taking his time to bring her to the peak of arousal all the while teasing her with the jargon of a serious doctor conducting a physical exam. When she could take no more he pronounced her well and truly healed, capable of resuming any and all activities of her normal life, and entered her. They clung together, moving with a ferocity that threatened to break Gavi's bed, and ended with a climax that caused Pholo to trumpet her release.

Afterwards, they cuddled in each other's arms, their trunks tracing lazy patterns over one another's skin. It was a delicate time, even for lovers who'd grown up together, vulnerable and exposed.

"Do you ever think about the future?" asked Gavi.

"It's all I ever think about."

"I mean *our* future."

"I do. You know I do."

"I know that all of our friends have long since bonded."

Pholo nodded and smiled against his skin. This was an old conversation, but it bore repeating. "All of our friends are much less ambitious than either you or me. We agreed to establish ourselves in our careers before we bonded, so we'd never resent anything we had to give up, and wouldn't lament having to choose between work and children. We're close, Gav, you know we are. You're up for that new position at the end of this season, and I've all but rebuilt my flight harness. And as my personal physician has just signed off on my physical well being, the next tenday of testing will allow me to establish my accomplishment to the university and they'll award me tenure despite my youth."

He rose up on his side and loomed over her. "And then?"

She pushed him down, reached over and found him ready to go again. She straddled him, gasped with pleasure as she felt him, and promised, "And then we will bond, I'll become fertile, my aunts will throw us a huge wedding, Bindle will cry her eyes out and toast us in verse, and we'll start the family we've planned since we were too young to know what it required."

"I'd love that," he said.

"You love this too, don't you?" She kissed his face as she rode him.

"I love you," he said, which was almost always the right thing to say. He knew it, and knew that she knew that he knew it.

"That's our future," she said. "Our near future. Until then, this is just practice."

The Dream

PHOLO RETURNED HOME LATE the next morning. Gavi had been long gone when she awoke, and she vaguely recalled him mentioning something about early rounds. The poor dear, she'd kept him awake far into the night, the smile on her face only slightly marred by thoughts of the patients who might receive something less than his usual level of care today, at least until he managed a nap. In sympathy, she allowed herself to sleep in, justifying it by her 'medical leave' status. When she finally arose, motivated by the rumbling of her empty stomach, a quick search of Gavi's room failed to turn up the ingredients of a decent breakfast. She didn't want to brave the rooming house's communal kitchen so she headed home.

All shifts of the house's morning meal had been concluded. The nieces and nephews had long since finished their chores and trotted off to their respective gymnasia for lessons. A hand of aunts puttered about laying out the fixings for a light nuncheon for any of the residents who might be showing up for a nibble. Two made *tsk tsk* noises when Pholo helped herself to an assortment of their preparations and one casually remarked that the dress she had on held up quite well into its second day of wearing. She bit back the scathing reply that came to her mind and made a promise to herself to *not* grow up to become like any of them. That thought put a smile on her face, made all the sweeter by the confused looks it elicited from the aunts.

Stomach satisfied for the moment, Pholo hurried

to her bedroom-turned-lab and set to work. The temptation to make changes to her design had been strong, but given that she had yet to perform the rigorous field tests she'd planned — ignoring the actual rigor of traversing a cyclone — it hadn't seemed prudent to alter things just yet. Which meant that she already had all the specifications for the required components and the orders she'd placed earlier in the last tenday had all finally arrived.

Day and night blurred as she worked. Several times she had to pause, when sheer cognitive fatigue caught up with her and the degree of focus she needed waned. Only then would she collapse on her cot for a fraction of a night's sleep or stagger down to the kitchen for sustenance never certain of the hour or the meal she might find. The regular rhythms of the house didn't apply to her now, and her relatives gave her space. As Granny Rosie had noted, she wasn't the first Pholo to live under this roof, and they'd all heard the stories of past namesakes. Had she noticed, had she been able to spare the awareness, Pholo would surely have been amused, but she had locked all of her attention on recreating her gear and flying again.

She didn't waste any time trying to salvage the original frame, she simply started over from scratch. It had meant tapping into her seasonal share of house profits — every adult woman living in the house owned shares in Salaphora's soup conglomerate and those shares paid regular dividends — in order to cover the expense of the materials. It was understood that such income was to be saved for a dry day, but given the beating the old frame had taken, the risk of microfractures had made it an easy decision. It was one thing to be frugal, but cutting corners on the fundamental infrastructure of her design would have been foolhardy. There would always be time to earn back the monies, particularly once she vetted her design.

Her goggles were a refit of a standard model used by the sailors of the archipelago's marine force, who sometimes had need of diagnostic displays in the midst of stormy seas, unlike the typical Fant who could go several seasons without encountering any technology more complex than an atomizer for watering orchids or a bubble filter for keeping the air out of a fermenting must. Admittedly, the displays that Pholo ran through her goggles were unlike anything the sailors might use, but that didn't matter.

The three stabilizing plates gave her the most difficulty. Each required a full day to calibrate and interface with the new goggles, and then another when she linked them together and the model they maintained fell into place in three dimensions. Strictly speaking, they weren't required to produce flight, but if she wanted to control her orientation while flying she needed them.

The tests she had in mind didn't involve anything as dangerous as her last flight, nor achieving altitude much higher than the height of an island's canopy. Strictly speaking, she didn't need to replace the silk flight suit that had been essential before. Still, it was one more variable she could control, and so she ordered a bolt of silk from one of her cousins who worked in textiles and spent two days cutting and sewing, recreating the one-piece and even the gripping socks.

Finally, the battery she'd braved a cyclone to charge had to be installed. It was the only piece of the previous flight harness that she'd kept and she snapped it into place as easily as closing the lid of a cookie jar against the nubs of a greedy niece who wanted more than her share. Raising the goggles to her eyes, Pholo initiated a quick diagnostic. All indicators came back green and the battery showed a remarkable ninety-eight and a half percent, plus or minus a two percent error — and after the experience in the storm she'd never overlook error ranges again.

In all, it required yet another full tenday to create a new flight harness. When she finished, she wanted to rejoice, but instead stumbled from her workbench to her cot and dropped into deep, dreamless sleep. She awoke the next morning in sync with the house's schedule and joined a packed dining room of aunts, cousins, nieces, and nephews for a breakfast of porridge and berries, spirited conversation, and vibrant good will that reminded her of why she worked so hard. Family. All around her was family. A greater miracle than flying ever could be, but discounted because it was commonplace. She wasn't about to give up on the flying, or the science that had led her to it, but it helped to renew her perspective. None of it would have been possible without the backing of family.

Having been doubled over her workbench for a tenday and forced to convalesce for two more before that, Pholo needed to get out, walk around, immerse herself in the life of her island. More cheery than they'd seen her in several seasons, she bid farewell to her aunts and wandered the boardways until her feet led her to the cul-de-sac of Bindle's apartment. Poets, as Pholo had learned, liked to sleep in. She let herself into her lover's home, slamming the door behind her and stomping loudly down the hall to her sleeping room. The noise had made no difference, Bindle lay in a pile of clothes, blankets, and pillows, head back, mouth open, snoring loud enough to wake the dead. Pholo reached down, pinched Bindle's nubs, and jumped back as experience had taught her.

"Wha? What? I'm awake? What's happening?" Her arms windmilled, her legs jerked and kicked, her trunk flailed, all in a ballet of violence that was guaranteed to leave a mark on anyone foolish enough to wake her.

"Get up. We're going to the bathhouse," said Pholo.

"We are? Why are we?"

"Because we can. Because I stink. Because I haven't seen you in ages. Because I have lots to tell you."

Bindle rolled onto all fours and pushed against the pillows until she had enough purchase to stand up. The blankets fell away, reminding Pholo that her lover preferred to sleep in the nude. "Give me a piece of that last 'because' again while I find something to wear."

"I'm ready to fly again."

Pulling a long tunic over her head she waggled her trunk in agreement. "Sure, it's time and more that Gavi said you'd need to heal. Good on you."

"No, not physically ready, which I mean, I am. Ready with the gear." She paused, uncertain if her lover had made peace with her fear and worry in the face of the knowledge that Pholo would not give up her dream.

By way of answer, Bindle swept her up in a hug, lifting Pholo from her feet. "That's incredible. When?"

"Tomorrow, if I can find a time when you and Gavi are both available. I have tests I want to do, a full day of them, actually. Distance and speed and maneuverability and the like. I already know it works, now I need to document the particulars for the skeptics. But I want the pair of you there for that first official flight. Can you make it?"

"Can I make it? In my head I've already canceled all other plans and started the first lines of a poem to memorialize the event."

"Wonderful. And we need to swing by and find out when Gavi can do it. But first, the bath house. I need a soak like you can't imagine."

Bindle ended the hug and smirked. "I don't need to imagine, 'lo, I can smell you. To the bathhouse!"

"To the bathhouse!" Pholo echoed.

"To the bathhouse," Bindle repeated and then amended, "by way of the pub, of course."

* * *

After several rounds of celebratory drinking and a luxurious soak, vigorous and soapy scrubbing, and another soak, the two women made their way to Kelprey's medical center. Gavi was just finishing up an obstetrics exam of one of Pholo's younger sisters' friends from gymnasium. Gone was the little girl she'd seen at some long past recital, replaced by a gravid young woman who looked ready to burst.

They waited while Gavi walked his patient to the front desk, handing her off to a technician along with a stack of paperwork. He smiled as he came towards them and Bindle leaned to whisper to Pholo, "If I were one of your aunts, this would be the moment where I said something about how wonderful that young woman looks, glowing with new life and such."

"You shut your leaf hole. I'll be pregnant one day. At least I like men."

"I like men fine. I like them best when they keep out of my bed. Besides, I'm a poet and my family is far far away. It's been years since I've seen a relative, let alone had to endure a knowing look or a disappointing sigh of 'if you'd only settle down with a nice boy.' Like that will happen."

Gavi reached them before Pholo could reply. He slipped his trunk around her upper arm and pulled her into a hug.

"Sorry to keep you waiting. Did I know you were coming by? Hello, Bindle."

"We're here to steal you away to dinner if you can get away, but mainly I want to know what time you're free tomorrow."

"What's happening tomorrow?"

Pholo beamed, leaned in so no one other than Bindle might hear. "Tomorrow I'm going to fly. I want you to be there to see me do it."

"Oh," he said.

"Oh? Just 'Oh?' Is that all you have to say?"

"Easy, 'lo," said Bindle, "I think you just caught him off guard."

Gavi glanced from one woman to the next and nodded. "Yes. That's it exactly. Um, as it happens, I'm done for the day. Let's discuss the details over dinner. My treat."

"Good save," said Bindle.

"What is there to discuss?"

"Well, I want to know what I can do to support you? This is the big moment, isn't it? Do you need any medical support? Any equipment for me to 'borrow' from storage?"

She hugged him in turn. "I just need you to be there."

"Wouldn't miss it."

"Great," said Bindle. "Then let's eat."

* * *

The next morning they assembled on the same beach where Pholo had intended to dazzle them with her post-cyclone triumph. She'd gotten there first, laden down with satchels containing her gear. Grinning despite the pouring rain. Gavi arrived next, having ignored her insistence that she didn't need anything and brought along a handheld vid recorder.

"What?" he said, in response to her frown. "We need to record this."

"Why?"

"To show our children how incredible their mother is."

That left her blushing and quiet until Bindle wandered down from the forest's edge and joined them on the sand of their little cove.

"Thank you, both of you, for coming. You're the most important people in my life. This wouldn't have half as much meaning if you weren't here to witness it."

"What exactly are you going to do?" said Bindle.

"I'm going to put on my flight suit, gear up," she said, and began to remove her dress with no notice or modesty, trading it for the silk flight suit she'd brought in one of her satchels. She stepped into the legs of it and continued as she pulled it on. "After a quick systems check I'll activate the flight harness, rise up, and fly from here to Gerd."

"Why all the way to Gerd? That's three islands away."

She eased her arms into the garment and closed the front. "Because I intend to fly down the boardways of the Civilized Woods of each of the islands between here and there. That should get some attention." The hood came up and she was about to stuff her ears inside but thought better of it. It had been uncomfortable during the flight before and she wasn't going so high that there was need. She pulled each ear through a slit on either side of the hood and then down over her head. "Then on the way back, I plan to swoop along the ports of those same islands. Oh, and I'll be dropping a few hundreds of these." She took a small paper card from one of several sealed pockets fastened to her upper arms and handed it to Bindle. It read simply:

PHOLO FLEW HERE

"When did you find the time to make these?" asked Bindle.

"Last night, after dinner."

"You said you wanted to go home and meditate before your big day," said Gavi.

Pholo just shrugged. "I couldn't sleep. And I didn't want to just stare at the ceiling. So... I made up these cards. I thought it'd be cute."

"It's adorable," said Bindle. "Isn't it, Gavi." She handed the card to him.

"It's more than that," he said, his voice going soft

and… reverent? "You're about to make history. Possibly the most significant event since we came to this world. And you asked us to share it with you this morning, to be a part of it."

Pholo had taken the components of her flight harness out of the satchels while he was speaking. She didn't reply, wrapping herself in silence instead as she worked. When she finished she sat down on the beach and pulled on first her gripper socks and then her gloves.

"I'm just about ready," she said and climbed into the halves of the flight harness and fastened the two sides together with a resounding click. She secured her goggles to her hood, and then pulled them down over her eyes. "Running final diagnostics check now."

A sequence of heads-up displays scrolled across the screen of her goggles. Everything checked out, just as it had during the tests of the previous days. There was no more reason for delay. She turned to Bindle and embraced her with a powerful hug that caught the other woman by surprise.

"Dare to be great," she said in the moment before Pholo let go.

Next she hugged Gavi, who hugged her back even more fiercely.

"Only you," he said. "Only you could think up something like this. Pull a dream into the waking world. You're stepping into legend, you know that?"

She kissed him and pulled back, grinning. "Then I guess you're going to be marrying a legend."

"I guess so," he said.

Pholo positioned herself a few paces away from

them, stopping just short of the water's edge. Lightning flashed in the sky behind her. Thunder rolled. It was time.

"If all goes as planned, I should be back before dark."

"What, are you serious? All the way to Gerd and back?"

She tapped the switch on her chest, powering up the flight harness. "I've packed the power of a cyclone in here," she said. "If anything, I'm going to have to dawdle a bit to avoid returning too early."

Her remark elicited grins from them both, which is how she wanted to see them before she left, happy, for her and for themselves, just in case something did go wrong. Then she soared straight up into the sky and the pouring rain. She was lost from view in seconds.

The Bonding

OVER OPEN WATER SHE FLEW, passing those few boats foolish enough to be out during the season of storm. From island to island she soared, over the harbors and up the winding ramps or parallel to the funiculars that led to each city's Civilized Wood. Above the foot traffic of boardways she slowed to mere breakneck speed. She tapped people on the ears with her trunk as she passed, delighting in the sounds of surprise, the gasps of wonderment. She scattered her hand printed cards as she went along, from one end of an island to the other. She didn't know this island, but there were patterns that were common to every Fant city: the placement of public amphitheaters, neighborhood spirals of commercial shops, and monuments of empty space amid the otherwise dense foliage. She soon found what she needed, a series of signs directing her to a memorial chimney. She followed their directions and soon spied an opening carved into the living architecture, effortlessly flying over the low wall that kept unwary children from tumbling into the chimney's shaft. She darted upward, rising through the curving vertical space until she reached its upper opening at the edge of the canopy. She soared through into the open air, leveled off, and accelerated to the next island.

Fast as she was, word spread. Outside of the universities, little enough technology was used on Barsk, but the marine force maintained a signal corps and had access to radios. These were sufficient to their need so that by the time she reached the island of Gerd a crowd had formed upon its southeastern beaches and harbor. As she drew near, she saw them jumping in place and waving at her. Closer still she could hear their trumpeting and shouting. "PHOLO! PHOLO! PHOLO!"

The flight harness worked to perfection. The diagnostics on the heads-up display within her goggles showed all green. Her battery had ticked down to ninety-seven percent. She looped through the air and slowed to a stop, floating above the largest group crowding the harbor's dock. She hovered in the rain, her ears flapping in the wind, and soaked up their adulation as they witnessed the impossible, a Fant who could fly.

They cheered. Heads raised to her, heedless of the rain, they pulsed her name in infrasonic rhythms that carried further than ordinary sound. At a flick of the controls she went from a dead stop and burst upward using the full power of a cyclone. In a heartbeat she rose higher than she had when she'd met the storm, passing through clouds. She was halfway to the stratosphere when the bitter cold signaled an alarm on her frosted goggles and reason kicked in. She slowed, stopped, and dropped, falling down with a similar speed to her ascent. To those waiting on Gerd's shores she must have seemed like a hammer falling from the sky.

She felt the harness strain as she pushed its limits, draining off her own momentum and inertia much as she absorbed the cyclone, pouring it back into the battery. In the end she managed to come to a halt nearly an ear's length above the crowd. They cheered.

Heart pounding in her chest, she mentally checked off that last test from her list, executed a lazy roll up and away, and headed back toward Kelprey. She began rehearsing what she'd say to Granny Rosie, how she'd explain this moment that would change her life forever. Would the old woman understand? Was it like that long ago day when Salaphora had crafted that first, transformational pot of soup?

Pholo flew towards home. At each of the islands between she paused, flew a lap around to the delight of the people who had braved the rains and poured out onto the beaches and coves for a glimpse of her.

* * *

The narrow beaches that wrapped around Kelprey overflowed with people who had come out for a look at the Fant who could fly. Pholo had anticipated some kind of reaction (though not to this extent) and planned a different rendezvous site with Gavi and Bindle than where she'd left them. Instead, they awaited her atop one of the observation decks that lay scattered along the canopy of any Civilized Wood. Unfortunately for her plans, as she flew over her home island's canopy she saw that all of the decks were packed with her fellow residents, all presumably hoping to view her as she flew past. She dropped down low enough to confirm her loves were in the crowd. While the others trumpeted and pointed at her, Gavi and Bindle only shrugged. What else could they do?

Landing as planned was out of the question.

Pholo flew back up and scanned the tree tops for a gap that would indicate one of Kelprey's six chimneys, seeking a shaft in the green that would at worst lead deep into the Civilized Wood and possibly all the way to the Shadow Dwell that was the ground far beneath the arboreal city. She plunged down into one as soon as she found it, hoping that none of her spectators would be able to tell quite where she had gone. The chimney angled slightly. It was wide enough to accommodate ten flying Fant with no risk of striking any of the lenses or mirrors that lined its sides bringing daylight into the city below. Like most such shafts, this one opened onto several balconies as it dropped and Pholo chose to alight on one of these. She deactivated and removed her flying harness, and disassembled it into its components. Next she removed the silk flight suit, folding it around the pieces of the frame in lieu of the satchels she'd used earlier. Then, naked and carrying a silken parcel, she ran down the boardway that connected the balcony with the other avenues of this section of the city. She got her bearings, realized that Gavi's rooming house was relatively close, and sped there hoping to reach it unseen due to the hour and so many people away from their normal routine as they sought to catch a glimpse of the mysterious flying Fant. If they'd only known, they could have gotten far more than a peek.

* * *

"Did you see the crowds?" Bindle asked, when the three of them were seated together again in the courtyard outside Gavi's home. "What I wouldn't give for an audience like that. And you say the same thing happened at every island?"

"Not every island on the way out, but yes, every one on the return trip. It was incredible."

Gavi sat with his arm around her, looking happy and abashed. Pholo wondered if it was their location. How many tendays ago since they'd last sat here and they'd both tried to convince her to give up her dream. But she forgave them and she wouldn't gloat. There was no need. She'd flown.

"And the harness operated as you expected? No problems?"

"Not a one, Gavi. I ran diagnostics after each test and procedure. Everything worked perfectly."

"Everything? Well, surely that's a miracle in itself."

She elbowed him in the chest for that and he responded with a laugh.

Bindle grinned at them both. "So what happens now?"

"Now," said Pholo, "I take everything except the battery back to my lab at home and run a complete workup on it and the data I recorded today. Stress analyses, power utilization functions, battery performance, and so on."

"You're not going to tell anyone yet?"

"Not until I have all the answers to the questions I know they're going to ask."

Bindle's ears flapped in disbelief. "How long is that going to take?"

Pholo shrugged, ears flapping. "It takes as long as it takes. A tenday, maybe two. I recorded a great deal of data today."

"That's all well and good for you," said Bindle. "But people are going nuts. Just on my way here I heard them asking questions. Who is Pholo? Male or female? Lox or Eleph? The entire island is buzzing with the mystery.

It's probably the same from here to Gerd, but more so here because people saw you stop here. They know you live on Kelprey. Do you have any idea how many people there are on this island named Pholo?"

"Twenty-two," she answered. "Or, that's what it was when I graduated gymnasium. I wanted to know so I went to the hall of records. That was over a tenyear ago though, so some might have sailed away or emigrated, or simply died. Others could have moved here from somewhere else, or been born."

"Yeah, well don't get too cozy at home. You can bet there'll be people tracking down every last one of you to ask if you're the mysterious flying Fant."

Pholo dismissed the issue with a wave of her trunk. "I'm going to be busy with my analyses. And one other thing?"

Gavi turned to her. "Other thing?"

"Well, sure. Now that I've done what I set out to do, and you've said the position you want is already waiting for you at the end of next season, I don't see any reason we shouldn't get married. Do you?"

"You mean it? We can finally become bonded?"

She kissed him. "I'd do it today except you know our families are going to want to plan an elaborate ceremony. Another two tendays at least, probably three. But like I said, my analyses could easily take that long. And when we finally do this thing, I want you to have my full attention."

"Fair enough," said Gavi. "But… along with your data analyses, don't you think you should have a very thorough physical workup as well?" He flapped his ears suggestively.

"To be sure. Probably several. In the interests of science, of course."

Bindle snorted and rolled her eyes, but if either noticed they gave no sign.

The Child

PHOLO'S ANALYSES ended up requiring nearly three tendays. Though she spent her time in her bedroom-turned-lab, her house was abuzz with preparations. Relatives from other islands were coming in for the event. Pholo's father, a respected vintner who had doted on her as a child but saw her maybe twice a year, had insisted on supplying a ridiculous amount of wine for the wedding. And her mother, a lawyer who nearly thirty years earlier had found herself ill-suited to parenthood and abandoned her to the care of her household before fleeing to a career in the eastern archipelago, had sent word that she would be coming as well, accompanied by a recent second husband.

Her aunts and great-aunts divided the tasks among themselves, meeting in committees and subcommittees and showing a degree of organization that would have put corporate leaders to shame. Lists were compiled, revised, abandoned. And everything, from the most mundane and foolish detail to the most critical, from who would have to sit next to poor flatulent great-aunt Mestpol to which of several family heirlooms would the bride trade with her new husband during the ceremony. One by one, all of these made their way to Granny Rosie for her final approval. The aged woman spent the days sitting comfortably in her hammock chair, armed with a length of ink bamboo that she used to sign off on each list, work order, and requisition. Otherwise, she gazed down at the yard, watching the children below as they played.

At first, during the chaos of wedding preparations, Pholo's work was continually interrupted by well-intentioned relatives who sought her input on this or that detail. She had tried to make it clear to everyone that she needed to focus all her energy and attention on her work, but not a one of them appeared capable of fathoming what could be so important. And so they continued to harangue her. Not a one of them believed the particulars didn't matter to her, not so long as at the end of the ceremony she and Gavi were legally married, culturally bonded, and ready to pursue a family. The constant intrusions during the first few days after the announcement were finally resolved by a simple sign on the door of her bedroom-turned-lab:

ANYONE WHO KNOCKS OR ENTERS
WILL BE *UNINVITED* TO MY WEDDING.
NO EXCEPTIONS.

Time passed in a whirl as Pholo poured over the data from her flight to Gerd and back. The battery she'd designed proved to be far more remarkable than even her most ambitious of simulations had suggested. The stabilizer plates had initially responded according to their software's parameters, but soon utilized their built-in feedback cycles to develop and refine heuristics based on her actual performance. And on and on. A pair of tendays? What had she been thinking? Three were not going to be enough to provide the documentation for more than a cursory writeup, and even then she still had to return to the university and her lab there where she had locked the flight suit's battery away in a shielded case.

For most of that span she left her room only to make quick visits to the kitchen or bathroom. The only other exception being that once every eight days she'd become aware of her own growing stink and acknowledge that her brain was going stale. Then she'd bathe, dress in fresh clothes, and go out into the world and learn the news of the day.

Her first outing involved dinner with Gavi, but she was too distracted to allow it to extend to a more intimate romp after. The work called to her. Early in her second tenday of analyses, she slipped away to spend time with Bindle. The poet had written a kind of epic ballad about the mysterious flying Fant who had circled several islands in the southeast of the archipelago, casting the anonymous Pholo variously as a portent of a brave new future, a parable about the Fant destiny, separated as they were from the other races of the galaxy, and as a metaphor for inquiry and the power of science over nature. Pholo was by turns agog, flattered, embarrassed, and simply confused by large passages of it. Bindle's eyes burned brighter than Pholo'd ever noted before, and if her work could inspire her lover to new creative heights then who was she to complain or get in the way?

Near the end of the second tenday, Gavi sent a note reminding her of the promise for a full medical evaluation. It was delivered to her by one of her numerous nephews by whatever lottery method the younglings currently used to assign household tasks. He trembled on her doorstep and wept openly after placing the slip of paper in her hand. The boy had surely read it himself and Pholo reread it several times, wondering why a de facto summons for a doctor's visit had reduced him to tears, before finally recalling the sign on her door.

"Hush, Küv, it's all right. The sign doesn't apply to you."

Young Küv, who couldn't have been more than four, snuffled out a mumbled "No exceptions. Granny Rosie said so, too," and resumed his blubbering.

Well, that was it. Her wedding or no, she couldn't countermand Salaphora, especially when the old woman was reinforcing her own request for privacy. And yet…

"That's true, but see? This note you've brought me is from Gavi, the man I'm marrying."

"So?"

"So it's his wedding too. He gets to invite anyone he wants. And I just bet that because you were so brave and brought this to me, he'll be sure to invite you himself and you'll get to come after all."

The crying stopped. "Really?"

"Yes, but… only if you don't tell anyone else about it."

"Oh. Okay. I can do that. Thank you Aunt Pholo." And he ran off down the hall, shouting to one of his sibs who for all she knew had been lying just out of sight. "I am so going to the wedding, Benjo. I am. So there!"

* * *

Gavi's clinic had the most advanced medical technology available on Kelprey, and while he wasn't the clinic's director, he had her full confidence and by extension access to all of the equipment. If Pholo hadn't known him all her life, she might have suspected him as some kind of sadist from the way he poked and prodded her, took samples of her blood and urine, skin and saliva. He peered into her eyes, her ears, her trunk, her throat, and then used devices to look around internally at her organs, her bones (the ulna had healed nicely), the lobes of her brain. He injected her with a variety of substances to trace her circulatory system and measure everything from the efficiency of her blood's oxygenation to the spread of neural activation in the different portions of her cortex.

Pholo was fascinated by the process, and likely would have been more interested still had she not been the subject of it all. As it was, knowing how thorough Gavi was apt to be, on the way to the clinic she'd made a stop at their favorite restaurant and arrived with a wide variety of take-away which they sampled between tests. As they fed one another, Gavi also fed each exam's bit of data into a central device that sorted and compiled the different components into a master diagnostic. Shortly before they had finished their dessert, the device chirped to indicate it was done. They gave each other the last bites, washed hands and trunk in warm damp towels, and sighed with the pleasure of a good meal in one another's company, both of them present and caught up in this moment that promised to define their lives together, the love they shared, the simple delight for each of being with the other.

Gavi reached for the device and activated the display. He'd already told her that, based on his personal experience, she seemed to be in perfect health and had sustained no lasting effects of her earlier injuries. The elaborate diagnostic report was a matter for the record and she fully intended to include it as part of her documentation of the efficacy of her flight harness, along with the stack of her analyses. As he flipped through the displays, Gavi nodded with each confirmation.

He stopped nodding. His ears dropped back and his trunk fell slack. Pholo reached for the device but he set it aside first and instead took her hand in his, real concern written across his face.

"Pholo, you're pregnant."

* * *

"Granny Rosie, I can't be pregnant!"

She sat on a low couch in Salaphora's private rooms at the center of the house, a space she doubted any of her generation had ever seen.

"Are you saying you've never lain with this boy?"

"What? Of course I have. Often and repeatedly, for more than a tenyear. And others beside him in the beginning. But none of that matters. We're not yet bonded. It should be impossible for me to become pregnant."

"You overstate the case, child."

Fear gripped her heart. Pholo had thought it, how could she not? Prior to bonding, Fant females, whether Lox or Eleph, were physiologically incapable of conception. There were exceptions, rare as the stuff of folklore, but real nonetheless. Exceptions spoken of only in whispers, exceptions that shamed not only families but entire communities. Was it any wonder she hadn't wanted to say the word? She had no choice but to do so now.

"You mean, an Abomination."

"That would be my guess," said Salaphora.

"But how? Why? Nothing like this has ever happened in our family, has it?"

"No, child. While the knowledge of such a thing would not be held by most of the house, I at least would know. You're the first of our line to bear this burden."

Pholo fought back her sobs. "What's going to happen?"

Granny Rosie chose to pour her great-great-granddaughter a cup of tea rather than answer. Through force of will she encouraged Pholo to drink it all down and then she refilled the cup. Thus preoccupied, Pholo's sobs trailed off. The tea pooling in her belly, the warmth of the cup in her hand, provided sufficient familiar ground to center herself.

"The first thing," said Salaphora, "will be discretion. Who else knows about your status?"

"Only Gavi."

"And how far along are you?"

"Three tendays," she said.

"You're certain?"

"Yes. That was the last time we made love. We were celebrating the success of my project."

Salaphora nodded, refilled her own cup, and eased back in her seat. "I know you have reasons for keeping your project secret, but perhaps it's time you shared some of the details with me. Everything else being equal, your success may be the proximal cause to your premature conception."

"I don't see how," said Pholo, a trace of a whine slipping into her voice.

"Well, let me tell you what I suspect, and rather than reveal your secret you can simply confirm or deny my suspicion. Is that acceptable?"

"I… I guess so."

"Fine. I suspect you are the mysterious flying Fant. That you're not a male Eleph as popular opinion currently believes, that the only thing the public has gotten right is your name, and that only because you scattered calling cards telling them so."

"There are other men and women who share my name."

"That may be, but you're the only one who has advanced degrees in both meteorology and engineering. I ought to know, I've signed the drafts for your tuition often enough. Plus, I sent one of your cousins to purchase one of those cards, paid a surprising amount for it too, I must say. They've already become quite collectible."

"That doesn't prove—"

"And I recognized your handwriting. Or would you have me believe one of the other people sharing your name also shares your penmanship?"

Any further protest died unspoken. Pholo tucked chin to chest, her trunk pooling in her hands. "No, ma'am," she murmured.

"So. Sparing me the details which would be beyond a simple cook's head, tell me how you did it."

"I… I ate a cyclone."

"You did what?!"

"I used the power supply from an earlier prototype to carry me into the eye of a cyclone, and then I absorbed all of its power, harnessed it, really. Stored it up in a battery I designed. Small enough to wear on my person."

"And why have you kept this to yourself for three tendays?"

"I've been running through analyses of the data I gathered. I only just about finished. My invention did everything it was supposed to do."

Salaphora set down her cup. "I would congratulate you but you've ignored the other side of this particular leaf."

"I don't understand."

"You say it did all it was intended to do. But have you asked what unintended things it might have done?"

* * *

Gavi had been waiting in one of the courting parlors, watched over by a trio of Pholo's younger cousins. They whisked themselves away like so much pollen when she arrived carrying a pair of satchels with the pieces of her flight harness.

"We need to stop at the university and my lab, pick up the battery there, and then go back to your office at the clinic."

"What? Why?"

"I think I made a terrible mistake. The radiation that shouldn't have been a problem, what if my methods didn't eliminate it all?"

"You said your simulations worked perfectly."

"Yes, but those were just simulations. No one has eaten a cyclone before and worn its power like a pretty bauble. We need to check my gear. If there was radiation, no matter how slight, we'll see it. The most likely source will be the battery itself, but I also need to check if what I thought was just routine wear and tear could be fatigue brought on by the energies coursing through the harness."

"And I'm coming with." Unseen by either of them, Salaphora had entered the parlor. "My presence may well provide some distraction from prying eyes. And too, I have a right to know what you may have brought to my house."

"Granny Rosie, of course, but... it is not a short walk to my clinic."

"Which is why a pair of older children will transport us there by cart. They await us outside. Shall we?"

They rode to the clinic in silence, Pholo and Salaphora sat facing forward with Gavi across, his gaze locked on his intended. Two Lox on the brink of adulthood grasped the long arms of the cart, pulling it behind them as they ran.

The side trip to her official lab didn't take long. One of her cousins stayed with the cart while the other accompanied her and carried the battery back in its lead-lined case. After bundling it with her satchels they sped off again. The clinic itself was nearly empty at this time of night. Whatever emergencies had come in had since gone, and only a single nurse and resident were on duty. Both waved to Gavi as he led the others to an examination room. Pholo emptied the satchels onto a table, laying out the pieces of the harness, the struts, the stabilizer plates. She unfolded her silk flight suit and laid it out flat. She left the battery in its protective case on the far side of the room.

Gavi approached with the same scanner he'd last

brought to his parlor to test her prototype battery. He took readings over each item in turn and studied the display.

"There are definitely trace amounts," he said, "but nothing worse than I would get exposed to at the clinic over the course of a couple seasons."

"Meaning no harm done to anyone at home?" asked Pholo, recalling Salaphora's lesson on family.

"I wouldn't think so, but you should probably keep the gear at the university from now on and stop using your bedroom as a lab."

"Agreed," said Salaphora, and that was that.

Next Pholo retrieved the case with her battery. While Gavi repeated his tests on this final component of the flight suit she packed away all the rest back in the satchels.

He presented his findings with all the solemnity of a much older physician. "It's off the scale, but the analysis suggests a kind of radiation unlike anything I've ever seen or heard of, though the outcome is clear enough. Based on these readings, its effects are slow and subtle but definitely mutagenic. It's a miracle you thought to leave it shielded and at the university. If you'd taken it home with the rest of the suit, it would have likely done harm to every growing child."

"But not the adults?" asked Salaphora.

"No, the disruptive effects appear to be limited to developmental cells. It would take a massive dose to alter an adult's more stable tissues."

Pholo spoke into the silence that followed. "Like I might have received as I flew from island to island?"

Gavi only nodded.

"Then why didn't we see the effects? If I'd been exposed for all that time, wouldn't we have seen some sign?"

"Not necessarily. Yes, there should have been some skin damage at the very least, but I could have missed it, or mistaken it for a lingering bruise from your earlier injuries."

"But you know what to look for now," said Granny Rosie.

Gavi smacked his forehead with his trunk. "Yes! I need to recalibrate and repeat some of the tests."

"Is she far enough along to assess the embryo?"

"Within certain parameters."

Salaphora stepped close to him, patted his cheek. "Meaning?"

"We know the date of conception. From that we can check to see if its development is in line with where it should be at this stage. Why?"

She patiently patted his cheek again.

"Oh! You want to see if it's, um—"

"An Abomination."

Gavi flinched.

"But Granny Rosie, any child conceived in the absence of a bond is by definition an Abomination."

"Let's not be so certain nor so hasty, child. There are many ways to make the same soup. Let Gavi run his tests. Information is like ingredients in the kitchen, the more you have, the more possibilities available to you."

The Lie

GAVI TOOK MORE SAMPLES, repeating all of the tests he'd run before, and others besides. The repeats provided nothing new, despite his reviewing them with new eyes. The new diagnostic tests were beyond the capabilities of anything on Kelprey, or anywhere else on Barsk short of the university medical school on the island of Zlorka. Pholo's samples were shipped there under a unique code string to protect patient confidentiality. Gavi and Pholo both memorized the code so they could retrieve the results once the lab had processed the samples, and then Gavi deleted it from the system. Regardless of the outcome, no one would be able to trace it back to Pholo.

Upon Salaphora's advice, the wedding went forward as planned. The house filled with visiting relatives and out-family guests to the point that even the children's sleeping porches were commandeered and temporarily sectioned off to afford a modicum of privacy. As for the former residents, they were sent with sleeping pads to the roof. During the handful of days before and after the wedding that defined the occupation, only one young cousin accidentally rolled off the roof and woke up in a large sarthna bush.

Bathroom schedules were a nightmare and the less said about them the better.

Pholo spent the final days prior to her wedding being ordered about and advised by aunts and great-aunts (and her mother once she arrived). More often than not, each bit of wisdom dispensed was contradicted by another piece, usually the same day, everything from how to keep her husband happy, how to keep him docile, how to keep him interested, how to keep him at bay. How much time to spend cohabiting, when and if to move back to the family home, when to take a lover. Names for children, number of children to have, spacing of children, methods for ensuring no additional children. Child rearing techniques, management of well-meaning relatives' influence on her children, dealing with instructors, teachers, tutors, school officials, and other parents who have their own surely incorrect opinions on her children's performance, abilities, talents, appearance, behavior. This barrage began during breakfast and continued on to the day's final meal. It would have gone into the night had Pholo not offered up her bedroom — after moving most of her equipment back to her university office and stacking her workbenches one upon the other in the corner up to the ceiling — for her mother's use. She fled to Bindle's apartment and allowed her lover to soothe her aching head with tender kisses and intimate touches.

Pholo assumed that Gavi was undergoing his own parallel ordeals, and when Bindle inquired of some of her bachelor neighbors who were acquainted with one or another of Gavi's male relatives, they assured her that the young man was occupied with manly rituals, physical contests of strength, toxic levels of inebriation, and a medical scavenger hunt organized by some of the other physicians from his clinic that by all rights should have landed them all in custody and weighted down with hefty fines if some highly placed members of the clinic's board weren't related to members of the wedding party.

The day of the ceremony arrived and everyone assembled in the largest amphitheater in Kelprey. Pholo looked resplendent in a gown her mother had brought with her from the island of Yargo, which her second husband took great pride in telling anyone who would listen (and far too many who wouldn't) the effort and expense behind the dress. Gavi looked dazed, both deliriously happy and like a man who isn't sure if he's awakened or still dreaming. The officiant was a former mayor of the island, an old friend of the family who, rumor had it, had proposed to Salaphora four times, first on the occasion of her applying for a vendor's license the day she opened her first restaurant, and again every tenyear on that anniversary until succumbing to a musth frenzy on the fiftieth anniversary and choosing to settle down into a mutually monogamous relationship with a personal assistant thirty years his junior.

The ceremony began with Bindle marching from the back of the amphitheater to join the officiant at the bottom of the stage. She waited for the murmurs of the audience to grow still and then recited a lengthy poem she'd composed for the wedding that overflowed with breathtaking imagery, literary allusions, and prophetic wisdom that promised happiness and long life for the young couple because they brought out the best in one another and represented all that was good in men and women throughout all time and space. By the end of it, the entire crowd had been moved to tears. Bindle took her seat in the front row and the officiant had to allow a brief span for everyone to compose themselves.

Soon after, Pholo's parents presented her to Granny Rosie, who in turn presented her to Gavi. Then pledges were spoken, trunks entwined, and in the end amidst much trumpeting and stomping of feet, Pholo and Gavi were married in the eyes of the law and bonded by the customs of all Fant. The outpouring of love and joy from the assembled relatives and friends triggered an emotional peak in Pholo, and her body responded with a one time hormonal release that unlocked her fertility, or would have had she not already conceived. Awash with more joy than she'd imagined possible, Pholo took Gavi's arm and together they fled, laughing, from the amphitheater through the Civilized Wood and down a gaily decorated funicular to a charted boat Granny Rosie had provided as a wedding gift. The boat took them through the rain to a neighboring island and a honeymoon cottage with more amenities than any young physician or junior faculty member could have afforded. A hand-lettered card awaited them amidst a chilled bottle of sparkling wine and two glasses. It read simply:

FAMILY IS
THE MOST IMPORTANT
OF ALL

For the next tenday they put aside all concerns over medical tests and flying, all thoughts of careers and advancement and friends and relatives. They celebrated one another in old and new ways, shared the last little secrets each had withheld despite so many years as lovers, and lost themselves in the promise of the future that lay before them.

If either gave more than a passing thought to the ill-scheduled life growing within Pholo, neither gave a sign. There would be time for that when they returned to Kelprey, when the results from Zlorka arrived, when they had to make decisions that might scar them forever.

* * *

The results still hadn't arrived when they returned to Kelprey at the end of the tenday. Nonetheless, Gavi performed another full physical and reassessed the status of the child, now grown from embryo to fetus. Both mother and her unborn showed up as perfectly healthy. That had to be wrong, at least in Pholo's case, else she'd never have conceived.

Having set aside their sense of dread while they honeymooned, they continued down that path as they began their new life together. Gavi returned to his clinic and Pholo to the university. Time passed. Pholo began writing up a research article describing the design of her flight harness, drawing heavily on the data from her analyses to illustrate each step of her accomplishment. She wasn't ready to send it out, not till she learned the final result of her desire to fly. After another tenday a coded report came from Zlorka. Gavi decrypted the file and took it with him to the apartment that the newlyweds now shared. He prepared a light dinner for them both and waited for her to arrive.

"I have news," Gavi said as Pholo entered the apartment.

"The test results?"

He nodded, holding the printed report aloft in his trunk. "You're perfectly healthy now. You shouldn't ever experience any additional risks or issues from this."

"If I'm healthy, how did I conceive before we had bonded?"

"I said 'now'. The radiation damaged you on a genetic level, mutating the mechanism responsible for preventing fertility in unbonded women. Now that you're bonded, it's not an issue, and the aberration is irrelevant."

"That's good then, right? If I'm healthy, then surely despite the circumstances of when our baby was conceived, it'll be healthy too."

"Maybe," said Gavi. "But, now that I know what to look for, I can do a followup analyses at the clinic. When you're ready, I'd like us to go there so I can take a tissue sample from the fetus."

Pholo frowned. "Won't that hurt it?"

"No, I only need a few cells."

"What will that tell you?"

Gavi sighed. "If the mutation was passed along to our child."

* * *

Trunks entwined in the adorable manner of newly bonded couples the world over, they stood together in Granny Rosie's private rooms.

"You have the results of your tests?" she asked.

"Yes, as well as a follow-up I did on our unborn child."

"And?"

"Pholo is fine. The mutation shouldn't have any subsequent effect on her."

"And the child?"

"It's been passed on to her," said Pholo.

"Her?" Salaphora's ears flapped once and fell still.

"We learned the sex while performing the genetic tests," said Gavi. "According to the simulations I've run, there's a roughly one in a one thousand chance that our daughter could likewise conceive despite not bonding."

"One in one thousand of producing an Abomination?"

Gavin winced. "Technically, yes, but the likelihood of the child having any of the usual deformities associated with Abominations is the same as for anyone, better than one in a million. The odds are that any child our daughter gives birth to will be as healthy as she'll be."

"Except those odds are going to come into play with more frequency because of her mutation?"

"Well, yes," admitted Gavi.

"And does it end there?" asked Salaphora.

"No, Granny Rosie. Gavi has run the simulations again and again. The mutation will be passed along to any of my daughters, to any of theirs, and so on."

"But this mutation, it's not something a routine medical exam would reveal?"

"No, you'd have to know to look for it."

"And otherwise, your daughter will be perfectly healthy?"

"Completely."

"Well, that's it then," said Salaphora. "The three of us are going to agree on a lie. And the truth will die tonight in this room."

"Granny Rosie?"

"It's simple, my dear. You'll carry your child to term. At that time, your physician husband will record that she arrived a tenday or so prematurely, but is otherwise fine. There will be no mention that she is an Abomination. The rules that would have us abandon her moments after she leaves your womb will be ignored. We will bury the truth of her nature, and raise her as a normal girl. And we will never speak of this again. Is that understood?"

Gavi nodded but Pholo's mouth gaped and hung open.

"Do you have a problem with this plan? Would you rather surrender your child to tradition, to be shunned by all right-thinking Fant? To be left in the public square to die instead of lying nestled in your arms?"

"No, of course not. But... My work," said Pholo. "I can never publish it."

"Oh," said Salaphora. "I suppose that's true."

"I don't follow," said Gavi.

"I've gone over the analyses. No system can be one hundred percent efficient. There'll always be the risk of reproducing the same mutation any time anyone uses the flight harness."

"But the mutation wouldn't matter for men, or for women past their bonding and with no further intention of conceiving."

"That's not the point," said Salaphora. "Pholo is neither of those. Releasing her discovery with the necessary warning would lead people back to her own child. They'd quickly deduce the truth. Your daughter will be born an Abomination. Worse still, she'll pass that taint on to any girl children of her own, even assuming they allowed her to live."

"But that's crazy," said Gavi. "Her work is transformational. It will redefine society. She can fly! We all can!"

"No," said Pholo. "We can't. Not if we want to have a family."

"But 'lo, I can't ask you to make that kind of choice."

"It's not your place to ask. It's my decision. Maybe you're right, maybe my discovery would have changed the world and summoned a grand future. But a child will change ours right now. No, not only can I not publish the truth, I'll need to falsify my findings and disseminate lies to ensure no one else thinks to go down the same research path and recreate my flight harness."

Gavi took her in his arms. "But... this is what you've worked toward all these years, it's why we put off bonding for so long. And to throw it all away now?"

In that moment Pholo wanted to give in, to believe her new husband was right, that her work would bring about only good. But... at what cost to her unborn daughter and generations beyond? She'd done what she'd set out to do, proved her premises, created a working prototype. She'd flown. Surely that was enough to sate her lifelong hubris.

"What do you always say, Granny Rosie? 'The soup of the moment can transform a life'? This is the bowl in front of me and I can already feel the changes."

"It's a trade, not a loss," said Salaphora. "Family for science."

Pholo nodded, swallowed back her sorrow, nodded again.

"So, we lie?" asked Gavi.

"We lie," said Pholo.

"When we leave here," said Salaphora, "it will be the truth. The only truth any of us will admit to for the rest of our lives."

"But what will you do?" said Gavi. "Science — meteorology and engineering — it's all you know."

Pholo managed a smile. "Oh, I can learn new skills. I learned to fly, didn't I? I can probably learn something else too. Maybe I'll learn to make soup."

Salaphora took her great-great-grand daughter into her arms. "I'd be happy to teach you," she said. "And when the time comes, you'll teach your daughter as well."

"Because I'll have one. Because… family."

THE END

Acknowledgements

The idea for this story started nearly thirty years ago, and is mentioned in passing as a throw away line in my novel *Barsk: The Elephants' Graveyard*. It's probably something of an indulgence to include a reference to a bedtime story and then years later sit down and write the historic, "true story" behind that tale, but that's what you've just read.

Along the way this novella benefitted from the insights and feedback of Tim Burke, Arthur (Buck) Dorrance, Sally Wiener Grotta, Barbara Hill, and Catherine Petrini, which is to say the members of Noble Fusion's Eastern Court. Seriously, you folks force me (albeit at times kicking and screaming) to be a better writer.

When I thought I was done, a trio of generous souls went through this story line by line and in painful detail found typos and punctuation gaffs and errors of omission that would have detracted from your enjoyment of the experience. Thus I say thank you to Dr. James Caplan, Mark Mandel, and Gene Weinbeck, for your efforts to clean up my mistakes. Any errors that still linger here are my own fault.

Finally, thank you to Valerie, who has been waiting for this story and the one that comes next. I'll get started on that one soon. I promise.

More intriguing Science Fiction from Guardbridge Books.

Soul Searching
by Stephen Embleton

South African police use a device that can track souls in a harrowing search for a serial killer. But when one's soul can incriminate them before birth, can there be justice? NOMMO Awards Best Novel 2020 Finalist.

Outside
by Gustavo Bondoni

Earth is empty of humans. This surprising observation stymies Rome and his shipmates, crew of the starship come to re-establish contact from the colonies. What could have happened in the 500-years of the non-interference treaty to vanish everyone? Journey through real and virtual worlds, discover buried secrets and suppressed histories, and question what it means to be truly human.

Pillar of Frozen Light
by Barry Rosenberg

Jonan's indulgent life on Earth is upturned when he meets Yerudit, a remarkable woman from a distant colony. He finds himself pursuing her on a pilgrimage across the galaxy; encountering enigmatic alien artefacts, haunted by a shadowy figure; and discovering a life he never realized he was missing.

All are available at our website and online retailers.
http://guardbridgebooks.co.uk